Whole
Slaughter

Henson shrugged absently, his face clearly showing he was perhaps a bit annoyed at not being told all the details of what was happening that morning. A quick glance at his watch, however, chased all personal thoughts from his mind. Noting the time, he announced;

"Gentlemen, it is eight fifty-five. Let's get moving. The Boss expects you on the street in five minutes. The truck picking you up will be here in twenty. The Boss is expecting a full fifteen minutes of slaughter.

"Let's give him his money's worth."

Have The Spider's deadliest enemies returned to terrorize New York City? Once again, Richard Wentworth must abandon his dreams, and his beloved Nita Van Sloan, to combat the underworld's dark champions! C.J. Henderson brings you the first new SPIDER novel since 1943—brimming with the brand of suspense and blood-curdling action that only The Spider can deliver!

*The return of the
wildest crime-fighter from the
classic pulp magazines!*

THE SPIDER®
SHADOW OF EVIL

***An all-new
action-thriller***

by
C.J. Henderson

MOONSTONE™

The Spider: The Shadow of Evil

Copyright © 2012 Argosy Communications, Inc.
All Rights Reserved.

Based on the characters
originally published in
The Spider magazine.

THE SPIDER is a registered trademark and is
the property of Argosy Communications, Inc.

Produced by arrangement with Argosy Communications, Inc.

Rich Harvey, Editor

Cover artwork: J. Anthony Kosar
Cover design: J. Anthony Kosar, Erik Enervold

Interior Book Design: Rich Harvey/Bold Venture Press

Copyright note: Much of the Prologue originally appeared as Chapter 6 of the Spider
novel *Corpse Cargo* in substantially different form.

The Spider: The Shadow of Evil
ISBN: 978-1-936814-20-6

The Spider: The Shadow of Evil
Hardcover edition
ISBN: 978-1-936814-19-0

PUBLISHER'S NOTE:

Published by
Moonstone Entertainment, Inc.
582 Torrence Ave.,
Calumet City, IL 60409
www.moonstonebooks.com
Printed in Canada

I am very honored to have been chosen to continue the adventures of the *Spider*.

He was, of course, one of the longest running characters from the entire pulp era.

He was, in fact, around so long his exploits thrilled *two* consecutive generations of readers of thrilling adventure.

If I have, in any way, done a satisfactory job in weaving this first tale, it is only because of the efforts of one man who selflessly took on the task of making certain I knew what I was doing.

He labored long and hard.

If anywhere the book goes wrong for you — that's my fault.

Where it excites, however, where it transports you back to the halcyon days of epic adventure, that is due to the watchful eye of:

RICH HARVEY

Writer, editor, designer, publisher, as well as my friend, without whom I could not have delivered this book for your enjoyment.

"The oldest and best known evil is ever more tolerable than a fresh and unexperienced mischief."

— Montaigne

"The evil that men do lives after them."

— Shakespeare

"There is no colder darkness than that found within the shadow of evil."

— John Raymond Legrasse

PROLOGUE
TEN YEARS AGO

"REMEMBER," the woman said softly, "I want every man finished with his job and off the train in five minutes flat. Tell them, Bolo, at the end of five minutes—no matter what—the Green Fire will be turned on again."

"You really mean that, Captain?" he asked.

"I do," the woman known as Captain Kidd's voice snapped harshly, cutting like a knife. "How long do you think a train can remain stationary on the main line without the fact being discovered? If a single man delays us, the trucks won't get away in time. Spread the word—when five minutes are up, the Green Fire goes on! The sooner we eliminate the inefficient, the better."

Then, as if her words had been a signal, a whistle wailed off in the distance, wailed twice more mournfully, and died away. The woman licked her lips, hands tight on her binoculars. The blue-white gleam of a headlight built a glow above the shoulder of the hill where she watched the bend. The glow brightened, the light's eye pushing around the bend, thrusting a brilliant finger off into the night.

"Now ..." the woman whispered breathlessly, her fingers clenching, biting deeply into her henchman's muscle-knotted forearm. "Now!"

Within the distant train, all was peaceful and quiet. The overhead lights were dim and the brown curtains hung heavy and dark, swaying now and then to the quiet rhythm of the speeding Inland Limited. The gray-haired late-night conductor walked slowly through the dimness, stopping a moment in the doorway of the men's smoker to take a customary glance in at the white-coated porter, busily shining shoes.

The conductor gave a contented smile, then pushed on along into the car proper and looked weary-eyed along the swaying aisle. Somewhere a baby, awake in the night, gurgled. A mother murmured soft, lulling words.

The conductor was still smiling, his ears filled with the mother's softly hummed response when, like the fury of Hell unleashed, the Green Fire erupted! It struck with the suddenness of lightning, like a bolt from a blue and cloudless sky. The dim, sleeping aisle of the Pullman glittered suddenly with a livid brilliance. Green-white chains of jumping flame stabbed out from the flooring, the steel coach sides, from every metal thing upon the train!

The old conductor's face twitched convulsively as the chained lightning of the killers danced in fiendish glee. In the smoker, the porter writhed upon the floor. In their berths, men and women and children tossed and jerked in the torturing grip of the incredibly powerful voltage. From one end to the other—everywhere throughout the doomed train—the green, horrible light wavered and danced.

Then just as suddenly, all artificial illumination faded as light bulbs burst one after another, the lamps of the train burning out. A shrouding darkness settled over the Pullman, leaving no sound, save the clicking of the rails and the small whispering creaks of the speeding conveyance. Then, the green-white flare leaped again.

The conductor and the mother and the child lay dead on the floor, electrocuted by that first fierce flash of Green Fire. Their dead bodies jerked to the stabbing of this new torture. They and all the cargo of corpses aboard were ready now for the eager looters, ready for the woman who waited on the hill, watching avidly through her glasses, her small pink tongue touching dry, excited lips.

From where she stood, she watched with mounting pleasure as her electric death danced like northern lights about the length of the oncoming train. The locomotive was aflame with it; every car had become a living, wavering mass of the spitting snake tongues of the Green Fire. For ten seconds more, a third flash of the fire danced; then a final darkness descended over the charnel house once known as the Inland Limited.

Still the unlighted train roared on. There was no sound save the steady drumming of the exhaust, the click and humming of the rails. The woman's fingers gouged her man's arm until her nails drew blood. Finally, however, the train slowed, brought to a halt by one of the villainous marauders. Taking her hand from her man's arm, the gruesome crew's leader cried;

"Go! But remember, in five minutes the Green Fire dances again!"

From all directions, men armed with flashlights and sacks went swarming onto the steaming train. Within seconds a crew labored within the mail and baggage cars, tossing bags, trunks and mail sacks into the waiting trucks that had backed up along the rutty, small road paralleling the tracks. They were not alone.

Throughout the train men worked with a furious speed, robbing the dead.

A girl of twenty-two or three lay in her Pullman bed, her gaping mouth leaking dry steam, her white round arms lying across the coverlet. Her left hand was a charred fist upon which sparkled a large diamond. Noting it, a small man grabbed her wrist and tugged at the fingers. When they would not open, he snarled with a maddened fury.

"Cut it off," said the looter next to him impassively. "You ain't got that long."

A knife gleamed and slashed the dead hand. The little man wrenched the finger back until the bone snapped, hacked at it again, then dropped finger and ring into the pouch swinging from his belt. Hurriedly he then skimmed over his victim's bags, felt around her body, under her pillow. A half-dozen others were busy working the same car.

Another yanked aside the brown curtains of an upper berth. An old woman lay there, a book crushed against her chest. She had been reading when the Green Fire struck, stealing her life. Diamonds surrounded by rubies dangled below her gray hair. The man reached up and ripped the baubles out of her old, pierced ears, tearing flesh—smiling at his treasure.

With only minor variations, the same scene played out in every car. Corpses were searched then tumbled in pitifully contorted confusion on the floor. Heaping piles of scorched, burned flesh were created everywhere from what once had been the living. A baby lying flat on its back, its legs doubled and crossed as if it still played in death. The body of the aged conductor kneeling grotesquely, face and knees upon the floor. A young girl sprawled naked in the aisle, her flimsy silken pajamas torn from her by marauding hands.

As the three minute mark was announced, the criminals went into a last-second hunting frenzy. Bedding was tumbled down onto the floors by the frantic, swift search for valuables. A laughing thug ducked out of a berth screaming joyfully as he displayed the arm of a woman, the hand rich with rings.

"Lose the arm, Chuckie."

Laughing at the suggestion, the brute lifted a heavy knife above his head and whacked down on the wrist. The knife dug in and stuck in the bone. He wrenched it violently, cursing, jerked the knife free and sliced down again. The hand came off and he scuttled gleefully toward the door with it in his fist. Bolo glanced at his watch, then shouted;

"Thirty seconds to go!"

As the woman's second-in-command leapt from the train and scrambled down the gravel embankment beyond, everywhere behind him his fellows hurriedly tumbled from the train. The locomotive exhaust barked and the coaches creaked slowly backward. Many men were already crashing through the underbrush toward the roaring motors of their get-away cars. Bolo toiled slowly up the hill toward the gang's leader. And, just as he reached her side, she gasped in vicious wonder;

"Now!"

At her command, the dread Green Fire turned the night livid again. Once more it danced and quivered in the air, radiating from the train in leaping sparks of green and white and violet blue. All who watched were blinded by the brilliance. For several long moments it continued; then, as sudden as death, it was gone. And, only seconds after that, so also were those who had caused the monstrous slaughter gone as well.

Bolo and his leader were silent for a moment as their car backed and swung into the road, roaring off with mounting speed. After they were clear of the area, the woman spoke.

"Millions," she said, her voice purring, dripping with lusting greed. "Millions and millions. And not a chance of being caught, as long as we kill all the witnesses! That was how the pirates worked in the old days. They killed all the witnesses and lived to enjoy their riches!"

The woman laughed insanely, her second laughing with her. They would murder many more, plundering their way to a fearful notoriety that would last for a while, until crushed, like that of so many, by the man known to the world as the *Spider*. Then, they would perish, as all evil did before him. And they and their exploits would be forgotten.

For a while.

NOW

1

"ANYTHING else, sir?" All of New York City's glittering set were gathered within the grand main ballroom of the Hotel Excelsior. The mayor and all the secondary politicians worthy of entrance to the event were working the crowd, shaking hands, holding court, smiling broadly to one and all. The city's major business tycoons were also there, as well as many of its scions of old money. The biggest stars Broadway had to offer were in attendance, too, none so haughty or removed from the world they would deign not make an appearance at that night's memorable festivities.

"Yes, Morton, my good man, get more champagne on the floor, if you could. I do believe I see empty hands."

The head waiter leapt to do as instructed, despite the joking tone in the voice of the man giving the order.

"Richard, old boy," said an older man next to the joking one, "I wish there was some part of you that could relax—especially today. Of all days. Seriously, look around this room, but not for problems. I do believe you will find everyone seems to be having the best time anyone could, given the circumstances."

"I hate to admit, Stanley, that you could be correct

about something when it would mean I was not, " answered the younger, obviously teasing an old and dear friend, "but yes, all right, I admit that things do seem to be going well."

Stanley, more formally known as Stanley Kirkpatrick, Police Commissioner for the City of New York was perhaps the only politician in attendance at the grand party not canvassing the room for loose scraps of possible career advancement. Still a well-tanned man despite both his advancing years as well as the indoor nature of his job, his neat, no-longer completely black moustache waxed to pointed tips, Kirkpatrick attended such events whenever it pleased him to do so. And, that night it pleased him to forget—or at least, put aside—his duties for once.

His still lovely wife Lona on his arm, the commissioner had suffered the indignity of formal dress, "putting on a monkey suit when there are better things to do," to not only allow his long-suffering "policeman's spouse" a glamorous night out on the town, but also to support his friend of decades, Richard Wentworth. Wentworth was that evening's host, a much-envied, but also often much-pitied center of the Manhattan social scene.

Just millimeters beneath six feet tall, he was a striking figure, a man of solid shoulders and chiseled features. Wentworth was handsome and brilliant, blessed with sharp, gray-blue eyes and a wealth of jet-black hair, which unlike his friend's, had not yet betrayed his age with even a single silvering follicle. And thus, since the only way any in New York would know he had reached the age of forty was for him to tell them himself, he had done so, throwing his own party in a style lavish enough to allow them to forget for a moment the horrible war waging an ocean away.

"You know, I have to admit," said Kirkpatrick, allowing his friend's jape to slide by unnoticed, "I have sometimes thought a fellow like you would never reach such an advanced age."

"Oh, please," joked Wentworth, raising his glass in mock-salute to his friend, "you're not going to start that ridiculous business of me being the *Spider* again, are you? Especially not after last year."

Kirkpatrick smiled, shaking his head as he admitted the days for those suspicions were finally over. The commissioner had good reason to do so. It had only been some thirteen weeks earlier, in December of the year previous, when Wentworth had been positively cleared once and for all of such charges. The reason for such had been simple. It had been then when the *Spider*, master criminal, had died, in plain view of a great number of witnesses, at the hands of Richard Wentworth, no less.

Oddly enough, the city had reacted to the announcement of the *Spider*'s death in a somewhat curious fashion. Yes, he was known far and wide as the most sinister of law-breakers. Grotesquely misshapen, appearing anywhere, out of nowhere, blazing .45s administering death in relentless fashion, he had slaughtered thousands over his years of notorious rampage, then marked their faces with his scarlet insignia to make certain all knew the deaths were his responsibility.

And yet, there were those who would defend him bitterly. Indeed, most any in the city with no political axe to grind would swear that the *Spider* was more defender than criminal. Yes, they would admit, murderer he might be, but who in fact was it that he had slain? What souls exactly were they which he had dispatched to the Great Beyond?

Demons, they would tell you. Monsters, their answer would thunder. Men and women who thought nothing of slaughtering countless thousands in their attempts to loot and pillage. When, these defenders would ask, did the

Spider ever slay an innocent? Name one, they would insist. Find a single non-deserving person to whom he meted out justice, they would cry, and our voices will be silenced.

But, none could do so, not even Kirkpatrick himself, who had done more than any person alive to try and bring the *Spider* to justice. He had done so only out of his overly enthusiastic sense of duty. Even when he had believed his good and dear friend to be the *Spider*, and known in his heart of hearts that the monster of the night the ink-stained legions had dubbed "the master of men" had always somehow seemed to be working for the forces of good, still he had given pursuit.

Often Kirkpatrick had wondered if his inability to bring the *Spider* to justice had been a thing part-and-parcel bound up in his loyalty to his friend. After all, the *Spider* had passed on more than one opportunity to kill the commissioner. Indeed, the masked man had on several occasions, taken considerable damage rather than accomplish such a deed, just one of the many things which had convinced Kirkpatrick he was right as to the true face behind the mask and make-up.

"But," he thought, lifting his glass to his lips drinking deeply, "it doesn't matter any more—does it? The *Spider* is gone. Done. Buried. Finished."

Kirkpatrick was just about to expand on his musings to Wentworth when the socialite begged off from their conversation. Someone had just come into view for whom he had been waiting. The commissioner did not need any of his police training or years of investigative experience to determine his friend could not be restrained from immediately joining the lady who approached.

"But then," thought Kirkpatrick, smiling as he did so, "why should he?"

The someone in question was Wentworth's fiancée of long-standing, the lovely Nita Van Sloan. When first they had met, she had been a slender girl of barely more than twenty. Now, a fully mature woman in her thirties, she was still slender, but somehow, remarkably—unbelievably— she seemed to all more beautiful than ever. Her deep-brown hair hung in clustered curls around her perfect oval of a face, a visage which still shone with a vibrant energy despite all the thousands of horrors she had witnessed; terrors beyond measure which she had taken in with her dazzling eyes, beguiling pits of icy fire which some would call blue, others violet.

She wore that evening a designer gown of a cream-colored silk which hung dangerously off but one shoulder. Modestly it crept almost to the floor, almost hiding her matching strapped spiked heels from sight. But, the dress's length was a deceit, one which could not disguise its decadent cut, or the bold way it clung to its owner's every curve.

As Wentworth approached his fiancée, her beautiful mouth slid into a smile which dazzled all within sight of it. She was, however, no more aware of the surrounding glances of male lust than she was those of female jealousy. All her concentration was directed toward her fiancé, as was his toward her. Taking her into his arms, Wentworth walked his love directly onto the dance floor, crushing her to him as he whispered;

"Nita, my darling, I wondered if you might have a theory on a problem that has had me flummoxed for some time?"

"I'm told I can be a quite clever girl on occasion," she purred into his ear. "It's possible I might be able to help. Present your conundrum, good sir."

"Well, I was wondering, why is it, do you suppose, that I ever, ever, do something as outlandishly simple-minded as letting you out of reach of my arms?"

"That, I must admit, is a very good question."

"Yes, I thought so."

Wentworth grinned as the pair moved across the dance floor. The band was in the middle of one of those modernized versions of a classic waltz, a piece with just enough bop to keep the youngsters happy, but with also enough dignity to allow their elders to enjoy themselves as well. Both superb dancers, Wentworth and Nita flowed between the rest of the couples on the floor, gliding between them with a grace that left those watching the pair practically speechless. Amused at the obvious glances, Nita whispered;

"I do believe the crowd is watching us, again, my dear Richard."

"Are they now? I hadn't noticed."

"Oh really?" Nita's words were a teasing accusation. Dropping her voice to the softest of whispers, she added, "I thought nothing escaped your grim visage, oh, master of men."

"Now, now, young lady," offered Wentworth, his eyes locking with those of his partner, flashing briefly with a cautionary reprimand. Still smiling, maintaining his mask, he said;

"Don't you read the papers, my dear? Listen to the radio? Haven't you heard? The *Spider*, that villain most base and foul, is dead."

"Yes ... I've heard that one before. Forgive me if don't hold my breath."

Wentworth knew he was being teased further, but he also knew something his beautiful companion did not. Months earlier, when the imposter pretending to be the

Spider had died at his hands, he had seen in a startling moment of clarity a chance to make a monumental change within his life—to reverse the seemingly unstoppable destiny which he had created for himself.

For more than a decade he had battled the forces of evil in the guise of the *Spider*. Starting out as a young man, driven by an idealism beyond most and a sense of duty barely incomprehensible to the majority, he had struggled onward as none ever before him. Living his life to serve an ideal rather than himself, he had fought and struggled to make the world a better place for all than any individual named throughout all recorded human history. Multiple times had he been shot and stabbed and left at death's doorstep, only to somehow miraculously rally and then fight on once more.

In New York City, in other cities, other countries, he had made the name of the *Spider* one feared more than that of Lucifer himself. And, indeed, why not? For the satanic lord of eternal Hell was only a figure that waited for wrongdoers—a superstition easily dismissed. But, the *Spider* was a real and solid threat—a cyclonic scythe that send such villains to whatever everlasting reward awaited all men.

However, after the years piled upon years of struggle, the rivers of blood spilled, friends lost, homes destroyed, the countless times his own needs had been turned aside, abandoned—shunned—he had found himself considering a disturbing truth: *what* did he actually have to show for it?

Three months earlier, standing over the body of the pseudo-*Spider* precocious Fate had delivered unto him, he had seen his chance to thwart Destiny. At one time he had hoped to make a difference, to be the forged light of truth which might somehow lead mankind to the greater heights it was capable of reaching. But, despite all his near-superhuman efforts, there was no arguing that the human race was in many ways a more pitiful species than ever.

The Great War, the conflict to end all war forever, had been a horror devastating enough. But, monstrous and unthinkable as its terrible excesses had been, the war ravaging Europe and Asia at that moment was a thing even worse. Indeed, the frightful, blasphemous things men were now doing to each other on the largest scale the race had ever conceived had made Richard Wentworth pause and wonder—

Was there any point to doing what he did?

In a world that could murder with such unthinkable efficiency, of what use was one man dressing up in the night?

When he had started out, he had been a lone hero struggling in a world of incompetent police forces and crooked judiciaries. But, other heroes had arisen. His good friend Kirkpatrick had struggled magnificently to clean up the New York City police department. Beyond that, between the two of them, they had swept enough of the swindlers and grifters from the legal system that finally, it seemed, the man-in-the-street might finally a chance. And, thus thinking, he had asked himself;

"Well, if everyone else in the world deserves a chance at what they want, then ... don't I?"

And that was when Wentworth had made a vow to himself. He would test the waters, wait the handful of weeks to his next birthday, see if he could go that long without once more becoming the *Spider*. At first he had expected such to be an ordeal. But, none were more surprised than himself when he discovered it easier as each day passed to leave his guns and bombs hidden within their secret compartments, to simply turn the radio off when it spoke of this or that crime.

And, as his birthday approached, he found himself growing overwhelmingly excited. When setting its date as a test, he had told himself what his reward for leaving aside the mantle of the *Spider* would be. More than once over the years had he proposed to his lovely Nita, only to then never find a way to get them both to the altar. She had stood by his side since the beginning. She had suffered terrible indignities at the hands of all manner of villains, had fought and bled and given as good as she had received.

"My dear, you deserve tonight," he thought, lost for a moment in the warm glow of her wonderful eyes. "And, so do I, for that matter."

If the band had stopped playing a handful of seconds earlier, Wentworth might have made the speech he had been preparing for his lovely Nita since the bloody day in December when Fate had attempted to finally reward him for all his efforts on humanity's behalf.

But, they did not.

The band leader, watching the dazzling couple move across the dance floor like none he had ever beheld, save on the silver screen, had actually slowed the moment, making their dance last longer, both for the crowd's and his own enjoyment—as well as theirs.

And thus, before Wentworth could speak, just seconds before he could say what had been on his mind for months to the woman he loved, Kirkpatrick crossed the floor, coming directly toward the couple. His approach was a thing direct and brusque. Reaching the pair, he reached out and tapped Wentworth on the shoulder. As he turned, the commissioner announced;

"Richard, seems as if I have a whale of a birthday present for you?"

"And what could that be, old friend?"

"I've just received word, on the outskirts of town ... something horrible." When Wentworth merely stared, Kirkpatrick added;

"The Green Fire has returned!"

2

WENTWORTH and Kirkpatrick stood in the bracing night air, surveying the quiet scene before them. On a set of train tracks leading South down into the city, sliding out of Westchester and into the Bronx, stood a late run passenger train—one filled with riders who would never again seek any destination other than the grave.

"This is hideous," mused the commissioner. Silver breath escaping his lips, he muttered, "monstrous. How can this be? How is it possible?"

"I don't know what to tell you, Stanley," answered Wentworth, his attention not so much on his companion as it was the detectives checking the tracks. "In the end, Captain Kidd and her pirate gang ended up as dead as their victims. Whoever staged what was done here this night, it would almost certainly have to be someone else."

Kirkpatrick nodded grimly. He did not respond, for he could think of nothing additional worth saying. The commissioner was not a man to waste words, to fill the air with empty chatter simply to hear himself talk. Besides, the only thing on his mind at that moment was a subject he did not want to discuss. Neither did Wentworth.

Both men had always dreaded the arrival of a night

like the one they were experiencing. The world had always known villains—scoundrels. Madmen willing to sacrifice anyone and anything to obtain their twisted, base desires. History was filled with the names of despots and tyrants, killers all, maniacs who raped, tortured and murdered their way to power.

But, even after the beginning of the Industrial Revolution, when science had become for many the new religion, still the world had followed along much the way it always had, until that was, the advent of the Great War. And then, in that planet-wide rush to insanity—suddenly— human life lost all value—for everyone. Overnight, it seemed, honor became a word without meaning. Cruel, insane weapons came into play, terrors undreamed of in any earlier age, hideous engines that were turned against men as if the end of days had arrived.

Motorized war wagons with mounted cannon roared across the fields. Flying machines which spewed bullets and dropped bombs took to the air. Artillery was developed which could fling shells the size of a man across the sky— shells which might explode on contact, or more hideously, release poison gases. Men were killed by chemicals and biological agents created with the best of intentions by patriots. Men doing their duty.

And after the madness fell away, the death-dealing arsenals remained. As did their creators.

Before long, on a regular basis fresh terrors were unleashed on a new generation of civilian populations. Man-made horrors such as the Green Fire.

"You see, Richard, look here." Kirkpatrick had walked over to where his chief investigators had been going over the tracks. Pointing down, he said;

"Just like the last time. Two stiff wires sticking up so

they touched the steel coaches. Three sets that keep the Green Fire on as long as they're in contact with the mains."

"Where are the others?"

"This appears to be the mid-point," said the commissioner. "Should be another roughly fifty feet in both directions. About fifty feet after the end of the train passes one set of wires, the locomotive runs into the next set."

Kirkpatrick had brought Wentworth out to the crime scene for more than one reason. It was true, of course, that Wentworth had been appointed to a score of different government committees charged with investigating various aspects of both the law and its enforcement over the years. His friend possessed a keen analytical mind as well as a sort of a knack for seeing connections where none other might. No, Richard Wentworth's presence at any crime scene was always welcome.

But it was not for this singular reason that Kirkpatrick had insisted his friend accompany him.

On that night, Police Commissioner Stanley Kirkpatrick needed more than a mere partner in investigation. He had many competent detectives under him which could have filled that role.

No—understanding what he was going to find that evening, Kirkpatrick had known he would need a friend.

Both the commissioner and Wentworth had dreaded the day when one of the terrible nightmares through which their beloved New York had suffered would return to plague its streets once more. After all, criminals carried the same guns, used the same knives and garrotes and explosives time and again.

Kirkpatrick had wondered fearfully all too many times...what would they do if the criminal hordes finally realized they could simply throw the same horrors at their victims perpetually? And now finally, after years of anticipation, he knew.

They would stare in tight-lipped personal dread, knowing all-too-well what they were going to find every step of the way.

Silently the commissioner moved toward the last car in the train stalled there on the tracks. Wentworth fell in behind him, knowing what was coming as well as his friend, but needing to see it for himself—again. Exactly like his friend.

The bodies started at the very edge of the doorway.

The two men stepped in over the first corpse, trying not to desecrate it more than it already had been. The fried meat beneath them appeared to have been a young man, most likely no more than sixteen. It was easy to tell he had been reaching for the door. Perhaps to toss something from the back of the train. Perhaps to simply stand and lean against the back rail, watching his point of origin race off into the distance.

Whatever the case, it mattered not. For now the young man, who less than an hour earlier, had existed with his entire life ahead of him, was no more than a statistic. One of more than two hundred people murdered that night. He lay on the floor with his pockets turned inside out. His left wrist showed a whitish band of skin where a watch had once rested.

His was not the only one.

The car was littered, heaped with the dead. Bodies were draped over seats, crushed under them, hanging from berths, stuck half-in, half-out of windows. No woman wore any jewelry. Earrings, necklaces, rings—gone. Removed. Stolen—all of it. There were no purses to be found. No wallets, no money clips, no money belts. Everything had been taken. Many older, heavier corpses were missing fingers, digits snipped off by bolt cutters. Tie pins, belt buckles. Anything of worth had been found and removed. Only the deceased were left behind.

The total was two hundred and fourteen passengers and crewmen dead. Two hundred and fourteen who now all lay staring out through eyes burned from their heads, mouths leaked smoke through lips burnt and charred. Two hundred and fourteen bodies that one could easily discern had been casually rummaged over as if they were merely bags of potatoes.

Those who had looted the train that night had done so standing in clouds of human steam, the stinking mist created by blood being boiled and skin being burned. Some forty-five minutes later, despite the fact the train cars had been standing open to the chill wind blowing through the city that night, still did the gagging odor of murder permeate the scene.

"What kind of men can do this, Richard?" Kirkpatrick waved his hand toward a random few of the surrounding victims, his voice a hard, brittle thing as he continued, saying;

"Not just the killing, but the looting, the glee of it. This damn car smells like Hell's waiting room, but you know, you can just feel it ... these bastards were smiling, laughing, calculating their shares, making jokes."

"What kind of men," answered Wentworth, "the kind you've stopped a hundred times, old friend. The *Spider* might have been out there softening some of them up for you once in a while, but you're the one who tracked the monsters down, pulled them from the streets, then cleaned their messes up after them."

"I know. But to see something like this return..."

The second car they traversed was in the same state of carnage as the first, and the third contained all the same brutalities as the first pair. But, when Kirkpatrick and Wentworth reached the fourth car, they found something different.

Something new.

That something was the bodies of what would prove through later investigation to have been a group from a private high school returning home from a field trip visit to an upstate college. The high school was one dedicated to the instruction of Catholic girls. Eighteen of them, as well as the two nuns who had accompanied them as chaperons, were what the investigators found. All of them disrobed, their skirts and robes and pants torn from their dead bodies. Their fragile limbs twisted and cracked and spread apart. Their blood everywhere. Their pale bodies filthy with the prints of beasts.

"Oh my God ..."

The commissioner's words hissed from his mouth, anger strangling his voice to a growling whisper. Wentworth said nothing.

There was nothing to say. Kirkpatrick's eyes had gone wide at first, but he had quickly closed them and turned his head. Embarrassed for those long past the emotion.

Wentworth, however, did not avert his gaze.

"Oh my God in Heaven ..."

Instead, he scrutinized the brutalized remains of both of the nuns, of each of their charges. Standing cold and still, his body an ever-tightening steel rod, he stared unblinking, soaking in each hideous fragment of the monumental horror the room held, telling himself as he did so;

"Do not for a moment try to comfort yourself with a cliché on the order of, 'evil has returned.' Evil has not returned. It *can't* return because, as even you can quite clearly see, it never goes away."

Standing next to Wentworth, his entire body trembling, shaking with a rage so intense the commissioner could barely contain himself, he repeated himself in the face of the new atrocity before them, hissing;

"And this—*this!* Exactly what kind of men is it that could *do* something like this?"

Staring at one last nude corpse, the smallest and most helpless looking of them all, Wentworth thought;

"Dead men."

3

"**Y**OU'RE certainly in a mood ..."

Richard Wentworth did not answer his beloved Nita. Instead, he merely continued to stare forward into the roaring blaze within his living room's fireplace. He was not actually watching the flames or their thin trails of smoke, of course. Rather, his attention was focused on a spot far beyond that which might be discernible to any other. Watching his unmoving form, certain she had at least a bit of an idea of what was happening within her fiancé's mind, Nita added;

"So, is there any use trying to talk to you at all tonight, birthday boy, or shall I leave you to your murky, and apparently, all-consuming thoughts?"

In actuality, the young woman expected to receive no answer to her query. She knew the moods of Richard Wentworth well, knew them as she did the sound of rain, or the rhythm of the alphabet. Which is why, when he did respond to her question, her amazement was so overwhelming. Not lifting his head from his hands, not even blinking, he asked in a faraway voice;

"Tell me, honestly, was it all a waste, Nita? Was every bit of it for nothing?"

Crossing the room, curling herself at Wentworth's side, the young woman touched his leg with one hand, arm with the other, offering him what little comfort she could as she countered his question with one of her own.

"What do you mean, Richard? Was *what* a waste?"

"All of it, Nita. The *Spider*. His great war—all the effort. The pain. The years of it, the never-endingness of it. Fighting, bleeding, suffering, and for what?" Wentworth went quiet for a moment, then turned his head, staring at his beloved as he asked;

"Ultimately, what use was any of it?"

Nita Van Sloan sat where she was on the floor, any response she might make frozen within her throat as her eyes fell into the depths of pain radiating from Wentworth's. The delicate young woman had pieced together his broken bones and mended his ravaged flesh after a thousand battles. She had watched him suffer and then heal from wounds that would have snuffed out the lives of any other man she had ever met. But, after any of his encounters with the forces of evil, during all their time together, she had never witnessed anything within him as she was at that moment.

Nita had seen the man next to her in a hundred moods—sorrow, anger and misery, exuberance and blinding hatred—so many more. She knew he could love, could be tender and gentle, could laugh, even be playful. But what she beheld within the man next to her in that singularly shocking instance in time, she found more than merely troubling. She found it confusing.

Frightening.

For, no matter what he had ever faced in the past, Nita Van Sloan had never once heard even the slightest sound of regret in the voice of Richard Wentworth.

Summoning all her courage, taking a deep breath, flooding her agile mind with oxygen, she asked softly;

"My love, what has you so upset about this? You've seen things like you did tonight a thousand times before. What was so different this time?"

Wentworth's voice droned up out of him sorrowfully, a terrible pain wrapping itself around every syllable.

"It's true," he admitted. "Every word you said. I have seen that which I beheld tonight before. In fact, I've seen exactly what I saw tonight before." And then, his face falling into grimace, his mouth stiffening into a hard, drawn line, Wentworth closed his eyes for a moment, then continued, saying;

"No, that's not exactly accurate. I've seen the results of the device that was used this evening to murder long ago, but then it was employed to merely slaughter. I remember what one of them admitted after the entire affair was over. He had admitted that the only reason they had killed everyone was so no witnesses would be left to identify any of them."

Taking another deep breath, Wentworth tilted his head toward Nita's, then said;

"Simple efficiency. Monstrous, but understandable, actually. However, tonight ..."

The avenger's mind played over the scene in the fourth car once more. In an instant he visualized the horror once more, every detail magnified. His teeth ground against each other audibly as his memory replayed the sickening sight—the score of innocent bodies and the abuse they had endured. His mind spared him not a single snippet of the monstrous degradation, taunting him with the images left for the world to find.

Continuing to kneel at his side, her hands holding onto him still, Nita struggled to keep the extreme unease she was feeling from her voice as she asked;

"Richard ... for God's sake, tell me—what did you see on that train?"

"I saw ... futility, my dear," he answered harshly—judgmentally. "I saw my life's work reduced to a disgusting joke. I saw, clearly and unequivocally, that becoming the *Spider* was a useless, childish notion, and that in all likelihood I have wasted both our lives."

Shocked, barely comprehending the words she had just heard, Nita questioned her fiancé, asking him to explain himself. The tone in his voice growing in bitterness, he said;

"When I met you, I was filled with an idealism that seemed to me then to be the answer to humanity's prayers. I was certain that one man, one good and noble individual, one who fought for the rights of others, who punished wrong, who warred against evil relentlessly, who turned away from all of life's distracting rewards and threw himself headlong into such a goal would be able to make a difference."

"But, you *have* made a difference. You—"

"No," Wentworth snapped, cutting Nita off brutally. Rejecting her comfort, he stood suddenly, walking toward the fire as he shouted, "nothing's changed. Except for the worst. Men are what they have always been, and more so—brutish, grasping and ignorant."

Taking the poker from the fire iron stand next to the fireplace, Wentworth stabbed absently at the burning pyre before him—for a moment. After prodding it for a few seconds, he then drew his arm back and brought the poker down harshly, one-handed, no longer attempting to bank the fire, but rather attempting to smash it. Slamming the firebrands within, sending sparks flying both up the chimney and into the room behind him, as the burning cinders slammed against his person and scattered across the floor all around him, he shouted;

"What was *any* of it for? Time and again we denied ourselves all pleasure to instead battle in the service of justice. And why—why did we bother? Men are more evil than ever, and no one sees the slightest illogic in that fact."

As Wentworth continued to pound at the fire before him, his anger growing exponentially, he shouted;

"But then, why should they? How could I have expected them to? Times change, but people don't. I would say that it's the same rotten little world it was when I started, but it's not." Flinging the iron poker away from himself into a far corner of the room, heedless of whatever damage he caused with it, Wentworth spun around, staring at Nita as he added;

"It's worse."

His eyes filled with agony, his head tilting oddly, as if trying to simply fall away from his body, Wentworth let loose a painful sigh, then allowed his voice to drop to nearly a whisper as he repeated;

"It's worse."

And then, Nita threw herself upward, dashing across the room to Wentworth. Grasping him, clutching onto him as if he were a loose timber in a storm-tossed ocean, she cried out;

"Oh, Richard, you damnable fool. Of course it's worse.

Men aren't saints. They're born wicked and primitive and knowing only that they desire pleasure. In every generation, if mankind has been lucky, one or two good and decent people have been born, sent to try and teach the rest how to live, to point the way out of the darkness."

Tears streaking her face, emotion shaking her delicate body, Nita dug her finely manicure nails into Wentworth's shoulders, pulling him to her even tighter.

"I know you're tired," she told him. "And you deserve a chance to rest—you do. So many times you've given more than most could imagine. No man in all the world's dark history has ever suffered what you have, endured so much, persevered as long with so little reason—"

Within her mind, Nita's memory flashed an endless parade of moments which had shaken her soul. She saw Wentworth stabbed and beaten. Bloodied. Crippled by bullets—shot in the arms, legs, the chest—so many times. An impossibility of wounds, a blizzard of deathstrokes, delivered unto him with a seeming relentless fervor, as if there was no other man on the face of the Earth to whom such agonies could justifiably be delivered.

And then, she remembered her own torments as well. How many times, a voice from the back of her mind whispered, had she been dragged off by one madman or another? How many times had she been stripped naked, roped and chained, threatened with dismemberment, violation—death?

"Have you not suffered as well," the self-pitying section of her brain asked her. "Has your endurance not been tested? Why doesn't he deserve to feel the weigh of what he has endured—after all, are you not as tired as he?

"Have you never felt it as well?"

Her body shaking, all of her strength suddenly rushing

away, deserting her when she needed it most, Nita felt her entire system weakening. Tears still streaming down her lovely cheeks, her eyes going red, her nostrils clogging, she blubbered aloud;

"Richard, please ..."

Wentworth heard the plea, and grabbed at its promised salvation with all the power he had remaining within him. Shame flooding his spirit, he clutched at the woman in his arms with the same ferocious desperation she had shown him. His resolve rebuilding him, dragging itself forth from the depths of his despair, he murmured;

"Oh, Nita, I'm so sorry."

"For what, my darling?" Feeling relief and foolishness at the same moment, Nita took but an instant to calm herself at least slightly, then continued, saying;

"For allowing yourself a moment of humanity? For once—just this once—indulging yourself, letting down your guard? And I don't mean here, with me. I mean on that damnable train. You went in there as Kirkpatrick did, as simply a man—a decent, honorable man. And you were overwhelmed for a moment by the monstrousness of other men."

"It's true. I should have—"

"No." Nita cut her beloved off once more, her voice taking on a scolding tone. "You did what you needed to do. You helped Kirkpatrick at the train because he needed you there. You were there what you always are, the man everyone within this city counts on you to be. And here—"

"Here," he said softly, staring into Nita's eyes, "I broke down like an old woman."

"You gave yourself a moment," Nita countered. "You took a good, long look at where your life and the decisions you've made have led you. It's your birthday. Traditionally considered a good time to do such things, you know."

Still holding onto his fiancée, still staring into the wistful delicateness of her bluish, violet eyes, Wentworth allowed a smile to spread across his face as he told her;

"I don't know what I ever did to deserve you."

"If you ever figure it out," she replied, smiling herself, "do let me know."

And then, neither of them making the first move, the lovers drew somehow even closer and kissed in the light of the fire behind them, ignoring for the moment the cautionary shadows with which it filled the room. There would be time enough for horror and fear on the morrow.

For that night, they had each other.

4

"RICHARD, so good of you to come."

Kirkpatrick rose and came around his desk, reaching for his friend's hand. As the two men shook, Wentworth answered;

"After last night, how could I not? There's obviously something sinister slouching its way toward us, and you know, boring life that I lead, I always want to be in on bringing something like that down."

"Indeed," responded the commissioner as he returned to his well-padded leather swivel chair. Comfortably seated once more, he asked, "all prepared for an intense day of sleuthing for the greater glory of New York City?"

"Can't think of any place else for which I'd rather put in an intense day of sleuthing. And, as for prepared, I think I might just be. Jenkyns refused to allow me to leave Sutton before he could stuff me with bacon and eggs, toast, coffee, sausages—"

"Jenkyns," asked Kirkpatrick with mock amazement. "You're still working that poor old man to death?"

"I have asked him on more than one occasion to put aside the mantle of butler and enjoy his remaining years," answered Wentworth sincerely. "Just the other day I offered to set him up in Florida. He looked me straight in the eye and said that if I considered living with alligators, mosquitos and orange farmers a step up from living with me that I might in all probability be correct, but that he was too old and tired to find out."

The commissioner laughed heartily, pointing a finger at his friend all the while. Once the moment had passed, the older man wiped at his eyes, then allowed his tone to grow more serious as he said;

"By the way, my apologies, of course, for taking you away from your own affair, last night. Damn thoughtless of me, really. But when they told me—"

"Forget it," said Wentworth lightly, taking one of the visitor's chairs on the other side of Kirkpatrick's oversized desk. "You said you brought me a birthday present. A spur of the moment one, I'd wager, but still—"

The commissioner held up his hand to interrupt his friend. Signaling the officer who had escorted Wentworth to his office, Kirkpatrick told the man to fetch the reports that had been written up by the detectives who had investigated the incident of the previous evening as well as some older files he had requested be pulled. Waiting for the man to shut the door behind him, the commissioner leaned forward conspiratorially, then said;

"Listen, I admit I didn't want to go out there by myself last night. The idea of one of these things coming back. Frankly, it unnerved me. But I started thinking this morning, this is not the tragedy it seemed at first."

"I agree," responded Wentworth. "In those opening moments I too saw a terrible specter on the horizon as I imagined a wave of these terrors we've suffered previously rolling forth toward our fair city, but as you yourself have realized, all the menaces we're thinking about, they were all defeated in the past."

"Exactly. I've already tasked the records department to dig out the old reports from the first time the Green Fire was employed. Everything we did to bring it down the first time is simply waiting for us to do it again."

"Sadly," Wentworth said in a quieter voice, "of course, it will mean more deaths before the affair is over. These kinds of things always do."

"But that's just it," the commissioner answered, "that's what the criminal mind never realizes. Yes, they can get away with this or that crime for a while, but in the end they're always going to be brought low—Hell's whistle, simply through attrition, if nothing else."

"It's true."

"Of course it's true. As soon as the inevitable pattern to their crime shows itself, as it always does, then—wham—that's it. It's over. We move in and they're ours."

Both men were smiling as a knock came on Kirkpatrick's door, announcing the return of the officer so recently dispatched. The man came in with some seven inches of overflowing file folders balanced against his chest. Placing them on the commissioner's desk as directed, the officer asked if there was anything else required of him. Kirkpatrick told him that would be enough for the moment, and dispatched him back to his normal duties. Then, before digging in, he depressed the call button on his desk intercom, telling his secretary;

"Janice, keep the interruptions to a minimum. I'm going to be fairly busy for the next hour or so."

After that, the pair split the stack into two unequal piles, the larger being the files from ten years previous, the smaller being the ones from the night before. Wanting Wentworth's keen mind working where it would do the most good, the commissioner gave his friend the shorter stack, hoping having all the facts written up and before him might shake loose some answer none noticed at the crime scene the night previous.

Chatter between the two ceased as they each opened the top file of their individual stack and started reading. Kirkpatrick was able to move through his pile more quickly due to the fact that his files were of the previous use of the Green Fire. The commissioner merely had to skim their contents, sifting the reports before him for those tactics which had worked a decade earlier when first they had tracked the criminals responsible for the weapon and ceased their attacks.

Wentworth had far less paperwork to read through, but the tougher job by far. His task was to remove himself emotionally from the horrors they witnessed the night before, and to look for anything that might betray the rouges behind the new assault. Yes, it stood to reason that their motive was most likely profit.

But, he asked himself, what if it was not?

His keen mind buzzing, the criminologist found himself returning to the hideous scene that had awaited them in the fourth car. Horrible, of course, it had been, but what if something else had been at work beyond the obvious? A memory tagging at the corners of his mind, he asked;

"Tell me, Captain Kidd and her gang, if I recall correctly, didn't they have a fairly tight time schedule?

Quick in and out to keep from being detected?"

"Right you are. Good memory. I just read over one of the defendant transcripts where they mention that very thing. She allowed them five minutes to loot the trains. Then, the cars were burned again, whether her men were out of them or not."

Wentworth said nothing, merely staring at the folder before him on the desk while he pulled at his chin with his left hand. Noting the intense look of concentration on his friend's face, Kirkpatrick asked;

"Have you got something already?"

"A notion, at least. I keep thinking about ... the school girls ... and their chaperons. Whoever put together this crime, they may have copied everything about Captain Kidd's mechanism, but not her style of execution."

"What do you mean, Richard?"

"Five minutes in and out. What we ... found in that room, such horror was not accomplished by men with only five minutes to act." And then, as an even more horrible idea sprang into his mind, Wentworth added;

"Unless it was done on purpose."

"What are you saying?"

"Men with only five minutes to steal all they can don't waste precious time if their primary goal is theft. But we're assuming loot is what this bunch is after. What if it's not?"

"I don't understand, Richard," responded Kirkpatrick. "What else could they be after?"

"I'm not certain, but the more I think about the scene in that car, the more it disturbs me. And not in the obvious manner. The report of the medical examiner here states that all the girls, and their chaperons, had been ... violated. There were twenty of them, Stanley. No one man, no five men could have accomplished such a thing."

"You mean ..."

Wentworth lowered his head, taking a deep breath as he did so. His nerves were tingling throughout his body, his sense of moral outrage boiling over, threatening to explode. Calming himself, forcing his passions to restraint, he finally lifted his head, meeting his friend's eyes as he said;

"I'm wondering ... was all that we saw planned? Did these fiends wait for just the right train so that they could not only rob, but assault our sensibilities as well? For that matter, what if those poor girls had been targeted, and the looting was only an afterthought, a cover to keep the gang's actual intent from being revealed."

"Jesus, Mary and sainted Joseph, and just what in all of Heaven would their *actual* intent be?"

"Terror? Fear?"

Wentworth offered the words quietly, his voice low and self-questioning. He stared at his old friend for a long moment, then spread his hands wide in a sad sign of dismay, adding;

"Why? What their motive might be for this, no—I have no idea. For that we will have to wait for their next move. But, the more I think about it, the more I realize that terrible scene was arranged for us to find. Created for our shock. Men that could perform suck monstrous acts do not accidentally travel in packs. Thieves sent in to loot do not suddenly throw aside—"

His fingers trembling, Wentworth curled his hands into fists, then slammed them against the desk, shaking the various files before him. His eyes narrowing to frightening slits, Wentworth stared at his friend, telling him;

"There's no way for us to know what they're up to yet, but mark me, Stanley. This bunch is dangerous. They're after something I don't believe we could even imagine as of yet, but we're going to find out—soon—I'll bet dollars to doughnuts on that."

"But, Richard," offered Kirkpatrick. "How can they spread fear or terror with what we saw last night? Crime scene photos were taken, obviously. But, no reporter was allowed anywhere near the car. The public will not see a hint of what happened, nor read a description of it. The press knows nothing of what happened in that car. My men were sworn to silence. Rumors might spread, of course, but still ..."

"I know you're correct," admitted Wentworth, sighing as he sat back in his chair. "But still, something doesn't add up. If we agree that what we saw had to have been planned, it seems like a great deal of work for what they must have known would have been a minuscule result."

And then, as if the universe had decided what the two men needed was an absurdly ridiculous coincidence in their lives, a knock came at the door. Knowing his secretary would allow only the most important of interruptions, the commissioner called out for whomever was on the other side of his door to enter. A uniformed officer came in, carrying an early edition of *The City Bugle*. Handing it to Kirkpatrick, back-side up, the man announced;

"Just a caution, sir, you're not going to be happy when you turn it over."

Stepping back to await any orders the commissioner might have, the man grimaced slightly, as if bracing himself against a coming explosion. Wentworth's eyes glued to the newspaper as well as his own, Kirkpatrick turned the town least reputable gazette over, revealing a headline and accompanying photograph which made both men's eyes go wide.

"Fear and terror, indeed," muttered the commissioner. Dropping the tabloid onto his desk as if his fingers could not manage to hold it any longer, he asked;

"We're in for it, aren't we, Richard? We're in for something terrible."

Staring at the over-sized splash headline, the single word HORROR plastered across the top of the front page, and at the certainly cropped, but still quite lurid, photograph beneath it, Richard Wentworth could do nothing but nod quietly. His friend, he knew, was quite correct. They were in for something terrible.

What that "something" might be, however, he could not imagine.

Little did he know that he, as well as the rest of the city, would discover what that "something" was all too soon.

5

THE MANAGING EDITOR as well as the publisher of *The City Bugle* both found themselves in the commissioner's office less than a half an hour after Kirkpatrick had been handed their latest edition. Both men were dressed down by the commissioner in the most threatening terms he possessed. Possible charges were lodged one after another, the list long enough to ensure that at the very least both men might spend the next five years of their lives defending themselves in court. In desperation, Martin Basilton, owner of the journal, a tall man with a thin moustache, turned to Wentworth, asking;

"You're a reasonable sort. Surely you can help us here. Point out that your friend is exaggerating somewhat?"

"You look to me for comfort over this?" Wentworth asked the question in a tone of utter amazement. Reaching for the paper, he grabbed it up then flung it at Basilton, shouting;

"This filth? You're lucky I'm not the Commissioner around here. I'd have you shot."

"We coulda done worse, you know."

Both Wentworth and Kirkpatrick turned on the speaker, Jack Stanton. The *Bugle's* editor-in-chief, he was one of the city's most outspoken characters, and the man responsible for running both the article about the desecration of the nuns and their charges, as well as the accompanying photographs. Before either of his attackers could speak, he shouted;

"And I mean, a whole lot worse. Here. Look at dese."

Pulling an oversized manilla envelope from inside his jacket, Stanton tossed it on the desk, then crossed his arms across his chest in rude defiance. As Kirkpatrick emptied its contents, the editor added;

"Yeah, take a good, hard look at what I had ta woik with. You tell me there was any way ta be more tasteful then what I done. Murgatroid, you guys should be thankin' me."

The commissioner and his friend went through the thirty some black and white photographs in grim silence. None of them held any image the two men had not seen—they had been inside the Pullman car the night previous, after all. But, each found something morally repugnant in the viewing, in having the ability to refer to the monumental abhorrence as if they were surveying nothing more than picture post cards from Atlantic City, or a collection of recipes. As the commissioner went over the photographs a second time—slowly, analytically—searching them for anything which might help identify even one of the perpetrators of the crime, Wentworth asked the newsmen;

"How did you get these?"

"They was delivered to the office." Before the

criminologist could continue, Stanton cut him off, adding;

"Look, I ain't no idiot—okay? You seen what we had, and what we used. We didn't go anywhere near what we coulda—all right?"

"You didn't have to use any of it."

"Now Commissioner, see here," Basilton threw in, "we had no choice. It was my decision to run this aspect of the story. Surely you must realize if we didn't, someone else would. For all we knew, every paper in town had been sent the same material we were. It was merely good business."

Both Kirkpatrick and Wentworth found their anger relaxing slightly. Basilton, they had to admit, was not what one could necessarily label a sensationalist. Many of his editorials had been cited over the years for their advanced insights, for his far-seeing ideas and unique attitudes. Often he was accused of being something of a socialist, but he struck most as too intelligent to follow the simple reasoning of the Marxists.

"Not only that," added Stanton, "but, I knew youse was gonna have us down here, so I had everything ready so we could come prepared. Like I brought the photos. Right? Ta show we're all on the same side here?"

"That still doesn't answer how you got the photos in the first place."

"I know. But, don't worry. I got that covered, too." Turning to the door, Stanton opened it, then called out, "Jerry, get in here."

In response, a youngster of no more than fourteen entered the office. Before anyone could speak, the editor told him;

"Okay, Jerr, just like you told us, now tell these guys." The young man looked from Kirkpatrick to Wentworth, and then back to Kirkpatrick, as he asked;

"So, like you're the police commissioner for the whole city?"

"Yes," answered Kirkpatrick, hurriedly collecting up the indecent images before the young man could see them. Covering the overturned photographs with the envelope in which they had come, he then asked;

"Tell me, Jerry, what was your part in all this?"

"I sell papers, the *Bugle*, you know? Got the choice spot right in fronta da building. So, this guy comes up to me, and asks if I wanta make a fin. I ask who I have to beat up. He laughs, then hands me a package, tells me to take it to Mr. Stanton. Tells me if I open it, Stanton'll fire me."

"Did you open it?" asked Wentworth quietly.

"It was still sealed when he delivered it," assured Basilton.

"Damn right it was," insisted Jerry. "Five bucks? I don't mess around when five bucks is involved."

"And," asked Wentworth, "do you still have this fellow's money?" When the newsboy announced that he did, the criminologist asked;

"Would you sell me his five dollars for six?" The youngster asked for seven, and Wentworth chuckled as they made the exchange. As he gave the money over to an officer, instructing that it be taken to where it might be checked for fingerprints, Kirkpatrick asked;

"Now, can you tell us anything about this fellow who gave you the five dollars, Jerry?"

The prideful look the youngster had been wearing when relating how well he could take orders evaporated. Lowering his head, shaking it slightly, he admitted;

"Ahhh, no sir. I'm sorry. I guess I was kinda just lookin'

at the dough."

"Think for a moment," said Wentworth. Focusing his attention on the young man, the criminologist asked;

"For instance, was he tall or short?"

When Jerry said that the mystery man had been about the same height as Mr. Basilton, Wentworth continued, working to jog the boy's memory. Was the man fat or thin? What color was his skin? His eyes? His hair? Did he have a moustache or beard? How did he dress? Did his ears stick out? Did he have bad breath? Any scars? A broken nose?

Some details the boy could remember, some he could not. But, by questioning him slowly and quietly, and by treating his answers as helpful and important, Wentworth was able to assemble a more than somewhat useful description of the man in question. The courier young Jerry had dealt with proved to be tall and thin, to have thinning, unkempt brown hair, and a somewhat sagging moustache that sat beneath a broken nose. He also had a small, crescent-shaped scar on his left cheek.

Kirkpatrick called for a detective and a uniformed officer, giving them his friend's notes and instructing them to head to the *City Bugle* building to question any regulars they could find in the area—Jerry's fellow newspaper sellers, local shop keepers, and the like—to see if any of them might offer more details. Then, after his men and Jerry had departed, the commissioner spoke to the newsmen once more.

"I commend your foresight in bringing the youngster with you. In a matter such as this, every scrap of information can be important."

"We understand, commissioner," answered Basilton. "I do realize our printing of the part of the one photo we did use, as well as the notes provided—"

"What notes?"

"They're in da envelope," answered Stanton. Hiding a grin as best he could, he said, "they sent the photos to us along with a checklist of facts. Guess you two were so busy givin' the peep show the once over you didn't even notice—"

Before the editor could finish his sentence, before anyone could react at all, Wentworth moved in a blur, catching the man by the front of his shirt and then lifting him off his feet so as to slam him against the wall. Releasing his grip, he allowed Stanton to slide to the floor as he said;

"Save your filthy insinuations for the editorial page. Like the commissioner, I give you credit for coming prepared, for having the sense to bring the photos and these notes you've mentioned with you, as well as the boy. But make no mistake, I still condemn the both of you for your reckless use of such material."

"Please, sir," interrupted Basilton. "But let's be realistic. As I pointed out before, if we hadn't used this material, they would have simply gone to another outlet. Someone wanted this story to reach the public, and it would have ... and perhaps, not nearly as tastefully as we presented it."

Wentworth turned his attention to the publisher, fixing him with a look so devastatingly cold Basilton actually found himself taking an involuntary step backward. The anger pulsating across the criminologist's face made both the newsmen shudder. It also silenced any further complaints either might have felt like expressing.

Seizing the moment, Kirkpatrick called for a pair of detectives. Taking the envelope and its photos, the commissioner pulled free the several sheets of notes which they had previously missed. Then, he quickly filled the detectives in on what had transpired between himself and the newsmen, instructing them to question Basilton and Stanton further. Once the four had departed, Kirkpatrick turned his attention to the notes.

He read them quickly, passing the pages one at a time to Wentworth as he finished them. When both had gone over all of them, they compared their thoughts on what they had read, deciding there was nothing included within them which might help them solve the case. The wording was concise, the pages typed, the paper ordinary. Neither Kirkpatrick nor Wentworth saw much hope the physical evidence they were holding would provide much in the way of clues.

"Bastards," snarled the commissioner, pointing at the trio of pages there on his desk. "Care to wager there isn't a single fingerprint that isn't Jack Stanton's to be found on any of this mess?"

"I don't keep my bank account intact by taking such pointless wagers," answered Wentworth, allowing himself the tiniest of smiles.

"Probably wasted that dollar on the boy," answered Kirkpatrick, his smile equally small.

"Still, we have a bit of a lead, perhaps a clue or two in the photos and these sheets, but ... we also have something else."

"I'm listening."

Wentworth pursed his lips, taking in a deep breath through his nose. Looking across his friend's desk, he allowed the fingers of one of his hands to drum absently against its surface as he finally said;

"What I was saying earlier, about fear and terror, the idea that these people might indeed be dangerous, I want to add to that. I'd stake my life that they knew those girls were going to be on that train. What was done to those poor young women was definitely planned."

"My dear God," answered Kirkpatrick, snapping his fingers as he did so, "the photos."

"Exactly."

"They had cameras with them. They were ready to ... why else, unless ... they meant to ..."

"Yes," added Wentworth quietly. "But there's more. This also means they have their own dark room. These people are organized, Stanley. They took the photos, developed them, and had someone on the street early enough to deliver them that a special morning edition could be printed."

Kirkpatrick nodded silently, the full extent of what he was being told sinking into his brain. Whomever it was they were up against, they were smart, efficient, and ruthless. They were not simply thieves, common criminals. Monster they might be, but they were well organized, intelligent ones.

"So far, they've been ahead of us every step," added Wentworth. "They've got a plan, and they're obviously going to stick to it."

The commissioner sat behind his desk, lost in thought. His head continued to nod ever so slightly as his friend spoke, and for some time after. Finally, however, the slightly glazed look in his eyes faded, and he said;

"Still, we have our own plan. Like last time, we can set eyes to watching all the local trains, monitor lonely stretches of track. Check out truck rental agencies. Start compiling lists of what was stolen from the victims families, start canvassing the pawnshops, check with fences ..."

"Heaven only knows how far ahead they've planned," said Wentworth. "But no criminal plan ever holds together for long. We beat the Green Fire once. We'll do it again."

Smiling, Kirkpatrick stood, announcing that the two of them had endured more than enough for one morning and that they should go forth to find themselves some lunch. Agreeing, Wentworth suggested a spot he knew to be one of his old friend's favorites. In minutes the two had descended to the police garage beneath the building and ordered the commissioner's driver to head uptown to 42nd Street.

Oddly, the pair hit such unusually heavy traffic they were greatly delayed in reaching their restaurant. Part of it was due to the fact that, even though it was mid-March, the streets were still a bit icy. Still, after a while Kirkpatrick had given in and ordered his driver to use the car's lights and siren to clear a path, even though the only emergency before them was the possibility of losing their reservation.

It was, indeed, a fortunate occurrence for the two men that he did so, however, for if they had arrived even five minutes later, they might have died with everyone else.

6

"WELL NOW," mused Wentworth, staring up into the sky, "that's damn unusual."

The criminologist and Kirkpatrick had just exited the commissioner's car, ready to enter Rosanti's, one of their favorite Italian restaurants from the hundreds to be found throughout the city, when something captured not only their attention, but that of everyone in the street. Being at the mouth of Manhattan's fabled Time Square as they were, they arrived just in time to witness a spectacular air show. Three planes—one traveling down Broadway, one traveling up Seventh Avenue, the last roaring east to west across 42nd Street—came within inches of each other, to the delight of the crowd.

No one suspected that the display was anything but an entertainment of some sort. For one thing, each plane was releasing a vast plume of colored smoke—one red, one white, and, of course, one blue. For another, the planes repeated the action, performing barrel rolls while they did so, before flying off. Everywhere New Yorkers cheered for the sight. With the European and Asian wars not going particularly well, such a display was inspiring to them— bolstering of soul and spirit.

Men and women alike shouted and screamed and clapped their hands, their chores and errands momentarily forgotten as they revelled in their good fortune. The event had not been announced in the papers or on the radio. There had been no fliers distributed, no posters in the subway, announcements plastered to street lamps or building fronts. In the minds of the witnesses, it was simply one of those rare, wonderful things which happened in New York City, one of the pluses for living in the greatest city in the world.

Even Wentworth had enjoyed the spectacle. He was a patriotic man who loved his country and had given over much of his life to defending the ideals of its constitution. Such sights—simple as they might be—were as inspiring to him as to any other man or boy in the street. But, as he watched the crowd cheer, took note of the hundreds hanging out of windows, waving their arms and shouting, a thought hit his mind that soured his entire mood.

For a flashing second, he cursed himself for not being able to simply enjoy a moment like those around him. The color, the spontaneous gaiety, the surprise.

"Yes but," he told himself, his great analytical mind springing to life, "look at the smoke. Observe the way it's settling to the ground. The mixture they use for these kinds of displays ... isn't it suppose to dissipate on the wind?"

As Wentworth watched the red, white and blue mist settle into the streets, a part of his mind wanted to scream for people to run. Even though his conscious mind could not fathom why they should do so, every particle of his finely honed instincts told him something was wrong. And then, against any outcome for which he could have wished, the result the back of his mind had deduced played out before him.

The first to feel the effects was an overweight man, somewhere between fifty and sixty years in age. He was just lighting a cigarette as the descending wave of blue mist wrapped itself around him. Having just come up out of the subway, he inhaled deeply, greedily sucking down his first drag as if he had been waiting years for that moment. He did not get to take a second.

Halfway through exhaling the smoke he had taken in, the overweight man began to gag. He began coughing so harshly he drew the attention of everyone for thirty yards in every direction. The sound of it was loud, gagging—filled with a nasty gurgling so obviously signalling what was coming next that all those around the man backed away from him immediately.

Their decision proved to be wise. Only seconds after he had begun choking, the overweight man suddenly made a new sound, a dense noise which was followed by a shower of sputum. Several waves of vomitus bile flew from the man's mouth as he fell first to his knees, and then to his side. All around him people stared and shouted, backing further away as he began to thrash uncontrollably, bleeding from the mouth, nose and eyes.

"Good Lord," exclaimed Kirkpatrick, as startled as any of the others in the area by the sight just across the street from him. "What in Heaven's name is wrong with him?"

"Quickly, Stanley," snapped Wentworth, pushing his friend toward the door of the restaurant, "inside—*now!*"

The commissioner stumbled as Wentworth shoved him roughly through the doors of Rosanti's. Then, as soon as they were inside, he tore off his jacket, stuffing it along the bottom of the door even as he shouted at the maître de;

"Quickly, the windows. If any are open, even a crack—shut them. Shut them all!"

As he stole a table cloth from the nearest table, sending its plates, place settings and the such flying to the floor so he might use it to seal the other openings around the doorway, outside more people had begun to fall victim to whatever had struck down the overweight man.

At first the patrons of Rosanti's had been shocked by the antics of the man near the front door. But it did not take long for their attention to be drawn to what was happening on the other side of the restaurant's large front windows. Already a score of people could be seen sprawled in twisted heaps, limbs twitching—jerking erratically in the obvious throes of death.

Men and women, old and young, everywhere they looked the luncheon crowd of Rosanti's could see people hacking and screaming, keeling over, falling into pools of their own spew and blood, begging for help that could never come in time. Some managed to crawl a few feet, maybe even several yards, but in the end all of them finally succumbed, crumpling—dying as they gagged on their own fluids.

Realizing there was nothing more he could do at the moment, Wentworth coldly turned his attention to what was happening outside. Studying the scene, watching the crowd so he might understand exactly what was happening, his keen mind began to notice certain facts.

For one, not everyone who fell to the ground had been smoking. A few had been, but most had not. The second thing which caught the criminologist's attention was that all of those being slain before his eyes had been touched by the fumes from the planes. It did not matter which color of smoke they inhaled, or in what combinations—after only a moment's study Wentworth was positive, everyone that was dying outside had breathed in at least one of the colored smokes.

But, the third thing he noted he found the most significant. Although it took a few extra seconds for him to realize it, the fact did finally jump out at Wentworth that not everyone who breathed in one or more of the colored smokes was being affected by them. Although the terror which was burning through the crowd was doing so with ruthless efficiency, not everyone who took in the deadly fumes was dying.

And, when that fact finally made itself clear to Wentworth, he discovered a deep and terrible anger growing within him. Indeed, so obvious was it that his mood had changed from a shocked concern to a barely controllable rage, Kirkpatrick touched him on the arm, asking;

"Richard, my God, man—what is it?"

Outside, people ran screaming in all directions. At least, those who could move did so. For many others, however, neither running nor screaming was possible any more.

"What's going on out there, Stanley ..."

The restaurant crowd gasped, everyone taking a backward step as a smartly dressed woman fell forward against the large, central plate-glass window of Rosanti's. Luckily for all within the thick pane held firm. However, the diners had no thoughts about their good fortune as they watched the chic young lady slide down the glass, leaving several smearing trails of blood as she did so. Her weak clawing at the window, her feeble attempt to stand only gave those inside a chance to look into her eyes—to see their desperate fear and confusion. To witness her death as her eyes swelled with blood and exploded, the force of their destruction pushing her away from the pane, sending her crashing to the pavement.

"We've seen it before."

And then, as the hideous cries from the outside began to fade, Kirkpatrick's brain caught on to the horrible truth his friend had already discerned. Such a terrible attack as they were witnessing was nothing new. It had fallen upon New York before. More than once.

"It's, it's ... whoever ..."

"You are correct, Stanley," agreed Wentworth, both his hands balling into fists, his mind screaming in rage at the thought he was as trapped and helpless as everyone around him at that moment, "this has to be the work of the same blackguards who struck last night."

"Then the Green Death ..."

Wentworth nodded sadly. His eyes still focused on the nightmare of death ravaging the streets before him, he answered his friend through clenched teeth, telling him;

"Yes ... the Green Death was only the beginning."

7

"RICHARD, you're alive!"

It had only taken Wentworth a few additional moments to find a phone and get a call through to Nita. Relieved to find her alive and well at home, he was surprised to have her react in the same manner. With only a few questions, the criminologist discovered the reason. Times Square had not been the only target for the trio of death-spewing airplanes. Indeed, given the sketchy details Nita had been able to piece together from the radio report to which she had been listening when the phone had rung, Times Square had been the trio's third target.

"They said planes were working their way uptown ... first they hit Union Square, then Herald Square ... oh, Richard, are you certain you're all right?"

Wentworth paused for a moment to smile, comforted more than he would have been able to predict by his beloved's concern, then told her;

"Of course. Kirkpatrick and I are waiting things out in Rosanti's. Do me a favor, though. Get on the line to Sutton Place. Make certain Jenkyns and Ram know what is going on. Have them spread the word through all our associates."

"You'll be working with Stanley?"

"I'm afraid he'll insist, and I think it for the best. Once we're able to leave, I'm certain he'll want my assistance analyzing the situation. And, I must admit, truth to tell—"

"There's no place else you'd rather be."

"Now that I know you're safe," answered Wentworth, smiling once more despite the grim scene outside the window a mere handful of yards away, "yes. You're correct."

"Who knows you better than I do?"

The pair spoke for another few moments, but finally broke the connection, knowing they each had more important work. Nita hated the idea of hanging up on her end—knew that Wentworth would not do so until he was certain she had fully recovered. And, in truth, she had completely regained her nerve the instant she had heard his voice—strong and reassuring.

Wishing she could cling to him for a moment longer, could simply turn her back on practicality and common sense and give in to her female nature, still she knew what was best for both of them, and for hundreds of thousands— if not millions—of innocents all around them, was for her to release him. To turn his attention toward the monsters ravaging the city.

After finally hanging up on Nita, Wentworth first made a call to police headquarters to report on Kirkpatrick's status, then returned to his friend's side. The commissioner had remained by the restaurant's large picture window, surveying the madness outside. After Wentworth told him what he had learned about the other attacks, Kirkpatrick noted that he had not seen anyone else fall for some time.

"Been timing the damn thing," he explained, his eyes darting back and forth from the scene outside to his wrist watch. "Almost two minutes now. Of course, not everyone that comes in contact with the exhaust falls." The commissioner paused for a moment, then added;

"Just like before."

Wentworth knew what he meant. Over the years two different criminal gangs had attacked New York in the same manner. Various products consumed in great quantities within the city—cigarettes, alcohol, coffee, others—had been poisoned. Some as straight out death dealers, others requiring a trigger.

"Could be," agreed Wentworth. "That first fellow we saw convulse. He lit up a smoke, got hit by the exhaust fumes, and down he went. I assume you still think the same bunch is behind this that used the Green Fire."

"Of course," answered Kirkpatrick. "Two old menaces suddenly reappearing back to back? I'm not saying that it couldn't be some manner of staggering coincidence—that is the definition of the word, after all. But, no ... it's beyond reason that this isn't the work of the same gang."

Some twenty minutes later the pair were on their way back to police headquarters to begin investigating their suspicions. Dozens of emergency vehicles had begun to swarm into the area after only ten minutes, proving beyond question that the effects of the airborne poison had finally dissipated. Kirkpatrick spent a handful of minutes giving orders, and then had commandeered a squad car to whisk himself and Wentworth back to his office. The two left the officer who had driven them with a lunch order he was to secure for them, hurrying inside to try and get an overview of just what had happened to their beloved city.

As Nita had reported, the radio had been correct. The planes had first hit the three major Manhattan cross junctures—Union, Herald and Times Squares. After that, they had roared up Fifth, Sixth and Seventh Avenues, spewing death for another sixteen blocks until they reached the boundary of Central Park. The plane releasing the blue smoke had then diverted to the left to run upward along Central Park West Boulevard; the red had gone right up Central Park East, and the white had maintained its course flying straight over the park itself.

The planes had then been brazenly abandoned in the middle of Morningside Park, just past where the usually quiet area overlooked the Cathedral of St. John the Divine. Witnesses reported that the pilots had been picked up by a trio of black automobiles. None of the witnesses had been able to add any kind of details beyond that one meager scrap of information. No license plate numbers, physical descriptions—nothing.

Beyond that frustration, however, was the more tangible problem of the staggering loss of life the simple, twelve minute assault had caused. By seven thirty in the evening, the death toll had been confirmed to have reached over four thousand people. It was a figure which staggered all who heard it.

Four thousand people.

More than four thousand people.

Preliminary tests had shown that whoever it was behind the hideous attack, they had, as suspected used a combination of both the previous attacks on the city. More than a dozen staple products had been tampered with—cigarettes, alcohol and coffee, as suspected, but also milk, bread, and various brands of soft drinks, chocolate and chewing gum.

Also as suspected by Wentworth and Kirkpatrick, the spray from the planes had been a triggering toxin. The color of the fumes had made no difference. Residue from each scraped from the nostrils and throats of victims had proven to be chemically identical. And, whenever anyone who had consumed any of the target products within—as best anyone could tell—the thirty-six to fifty hours preceding the attack came into contact with any of the three, death had been both swift and painful.

"What's the tally now, Richard?"

"Four thousand, eight hundred and seventeen."

Neither man spoke as the terrible number echoed through their minds. So many deaths, so many murders, committed so coldly. So casually. Lifting his head from the paperwork before him, Kirkpatrick said;

"You know, add in those slain by the Green Fire, and this bunch has already killed over five thousand people. Good God, Richard ... it's, it's simply staggering."

"I agree, Stanley. It's also quite perplexing."

"In what manner?"

"Well," answered Wentworth, pulling at his chin for a moment, his eyes showing he was lost in thought, "last night was simple to understand. Murder and robbery.

Unpleasant, but straight-forward. Rig the tracks, slaughter the passengers, rob them, leave. But, once you start to analyze what all was done, it wasn't actually all that straight-forward—was it?"

"No," agreed the commissioner. "Not if you add in the idea that they picked the train so as to have those young women to ... and, the idea of bringing a photographer, sending the pictures to that opportunist Basilton—"

"Yes, what on the surface looks like a simple crime actually proves to be but the prelude to a campaign of fear. Flood the evening radio reports and the morning editions with the idea the Green Fire has returned. Then, give one paper something extra so that rumors can begin to run rampant—"

"But Richard," asked Kirkpatrick, his hands spread out wide before him, his mind grasping to explain what seemed a bit of overwhelming illogic, "why the speed? Why not wait a day before releasing the photos? Let alone the planes?"

"Let's think about it," answered Wentworth. "Who knows—perhaps there may have been a time table to the potency of the products they rigged. Perhaps they meant to use the Green Fire earlier and got waylaid in some manner that ..."

As Wentworth's voice trailed off, the commissioner did not question him. Kirkpatrick had known his friend too long, understood that he was reasoning out some piece of the puzzle within his mind. And, after a few seconds, Wentworth justified his friend's faith in him as he announced;

"No. That's the easy way out. If we start looking at any of this as having come about by this bunch having made a mistake, then we shall be underestimating them. What little we have in the way of facts about this bunch shows them to be ruthlessly clever and efficient. We must consider that which we know about them to be solid. What we have seen is what they want us to see."

"I hate to admit it," said the commissioner, "but I think you're right. If that's the case, though, then what exactly is it that these bastards *want?*"

Kirkpatrick's question hung in the air like an unappealing odor. So far the unknown gang had been working at lightening speed. In less than twenty-four hours they had turned New York City upside down. Flooded it with fear from the tip of the Bronx to the southernmost shores of Staten Island.

The commissioner's runners had been reporting back to him throughout the afternoon and into the evening. Every corner of the city was overflowing with fear. The people were in a runaway panic, and neither Kirkpatrick nor Wentworth could blame them, for they were living in a vacuum created by their need to know that which the pair of criminologists needed to know as well.

What did this gang want?

Hours after their devastatingly successful attack, no contact of any kind had been made. No demands had been issued.

The Green Fire had been a simple crime, easily understood, compared to what had happened that day. The cost of setting it off had been minimal compared to the loot the gang had captured. But, as they had realized after the morning edition of The *City Bugle,* it had only been the opening act for that afternoon's performance. And, unlike what had happened on the train, that day's murders had taken considerable preparation.

Infiltrating the operations of multiple corporations, various candy makers, distillers, cigarette manufacturers, et cetera, must have taken the gang months to set-up. To coordinate the delivery of the multiple tainted batches to the city would have taken an incredible amount of planning and effort.

And resources.

The gang would have had to put forth a major investment of funds—finding the scientists they would need, purchasing chemicals, distributing them, paying bribes—the fact that they would abandon a trio of aircraft alone showed that they must be working with a massive amount of start-up capital. But again, the question was—

Why?

Both Kirkpatrick and Wentworth returned again and again to the irksome fact that now that the gang had proved their point, displayed their power, prodded the citizens of New York City to the cliff edges of fear and then pushed them over, why were they not doing anything about it? It was obvious they had invested a great deal of time, effort and cold, hard cash in creating pandemonium. In two, simple, brief attacks they had murdered over five thousand people. But why?

Why?

The pair spend more than another hour scratching their heads over their unanswerable question. Between them they could find no explanation to the criminals' actions. Maybe, they surmised, the gang simply wanted to let their overwhelming capacity for bringing death to sink into the consciousness of the man-in-the-street. To make them willing to pressure the government to give in to whatever demands were finally made, to start an exodus from the city so that it might be more easily looted, to gain some manner of revenge unknowable to the criminologists as of yet?

They had no way of knowing.

"As you must understand, it's something I hate to say but, Richard, I think we've done all we can for the moment."

"I share your hatred, Stanley, but I believe you're correct. Grim a truth as it might be, I believe we will simply have to wait until they make another move. I mean, the airplanes ... any word on them yet?"

"No," answered the commissioner. "Found the manufacturer easily enough, but no way to trace the sale. Dummy business concern. Same one used to purchase a great number of things used in today's attack. Abandoned now. All its officers counterfeit identities. Outside of that slight description given us by young Jerry this morning, we haven't a clue."

"Then," responded Wentworth, rising from his chair, stretching out his arms to release the cramping he was feeling in his back, "that's that. We have to wait for them to either make their demands, or attack again."

Miserable at the thought, Kirkpatrick nodded his agreement. There simply did not seem to be anything else they could do other than wait.

As they said their "good nights," neither man realized how short an amount of time their wait would actually be.

8

SEVERAL HOURS later found Richard Wentworth returned to his home. Sutton Place was a much envied home, a grand mansion actually built on landfill extending outward into the East River in the area of Manhattan's upper fifties. Designed to be boldly stylish, it was a triumph of the art deco era, a structure destined to never be anything but an elegant part of the island's eclectic architecture.

Upon his homecoming, Wentworth had been greeted not by his manservant Jenkyns, as was normal, but by his compatriot, Ram Singh, who met him at the front door of his home in his bare feet despite the considerable chill still in the air. A towering figure, it was a toss-up what most people might notice first about him, his overwhelmingly powerful shoulders, his snow white, always carefully wrapped turban, or his thick and massive black beard. He was to many, a frightening figure, his black eyes always seeming to be staring through any he met. Ushering his blood brother inside, he said;

"Jenkyns is helping Miss Nita set-up in the southern wing. She has not used her apartment here in some time. Apparently it is 'musty,' and not worthy of her presence."

Wentworth smiled, but said nothing. He knew his friend's attitude toward Nita was merely an extension of his belief system. As a Sikh, Singh believed women to be things without souls, placed in the world merely to be a convenience for men. Wentworth did not bother to argue the point with him. Even if he could somehow win Singh over to his point of view, he sometimes wondered, what would it really change for any of them?

"I assume she brought Apollo with her?"

"Of course," answered the great Sikh, his attitude softening considerably. "How could she not?"

Apollo was a Great Dane. Wentworth had bought him as a puppy for Nita when his career as the *Spider* was just beginning. The dog had often proved a fierce and loyal protector. Several times he had taken wounds so severe none had thought he could survive—none save Singh. Each time the Sikh had stayed with the hound, nursing it back to health.

Such was only fair, or course. Singh was cut from

much the same cloth as Apollo. A terror in battle, recklessly courageous, utterly fearless in the face of overwhelming odds, he had thrown himself into harm's way countless times in service to Wentworth's causes, and in doing so had taken more nearly fatal wounds than any could remember. And, as he had tended Apollo, never leaving the noble hound, so too would the Great Dane curl at the foot of Singh's bed whenever he had been incapacitated, refusing to move until the Sikh could walk once more.

They were, the pair of them, warriors born, and Wentworth had thanked divine providence more than once for both their aid and their loyalty.

"What about Jackson?"

"He is here, as well. Once the radio began detailing the events of this afternoon past, he came here directly. As well he should, yes?"

"Yes, my friend. This whole driving myself around town business has gone on for far too long."

"And now," suggested Singh, closing the door and securing its set of locks, "now it is time for the *Spider* to finally make his return into the world."

"No, old friend," answered Wentworth, not turning as he made his way through the spacious foyer, "the world believes the *Spider* dead, and who am I to argue with the world?"

"If I remember correctly, *sahib*, you have been one to argue with the world and its despicable ways at almost every turn."

Wentworth paused, then turned to face his old friend. Nodding slightly, he admitted;

"True enough, I suppose. In another time. But it's one that's passed. The *Spider* is something I've been fortunate enough to be able to put behind me. I would hate to think what it would take for me to unleash him once more."

The statement did not depress Singh too greatly. Years earlier, when he and Wentworth had begun acting as paladins of justice, at first his blood brother did so as any other man might. The *Spider* had been an identity developed over time. It was not the only alter ego Wentworth had used during their years together. He was, in the Sikh's opinion, the most useful of them all, however, and he felt a certain sadness in having to think he would never fight alongside him ever again.

Coming into his home's massive central living room, Wentworth found his other main operative, Jackson, waiting for him. Ronald Jackson had been Wentworth's sergeant during the first world war. He had become completely devoted to Wentworth during that time, and like Singh could now not imagine ever leaving his side. To the outside world he was merely the millionaire criminologist's chauffeur, on those days he even bothered with a driver. To Wentworth, however, he was a weapons expert, a skilled fighter, and a loyal friend.

"Welcome home, major," called out Jackson upon noting Wentworth's arrival. "Ducked death again, I see."

"Yeah, but it's getting harder all the time in this town. I'm beginning to think maybe it's time for me to stop trying to get Jenkyns to retire to Florida and simply head there myself."

"Please, don't even kid about such a thing. Florida? Good God. Why not New Jersey? Bucolic as it is, at least Jersey has seasons."

The pair bantered for a short while longer, but then Wentworth cut their conversation short, saying that he needed a moment to both get a bit of dinner and to think. Heading for the kitchen, he told the others;

"I'll need about an hour, then we'll be going out—we meaning you and me, Ronald. Ram, I'll want you here."

"But ..."

Wentworth put up his hand, cutting his friend off.

"I'm not expecting any trouble when I go out. Just want to get in a little reconnaissance. But, the way the past has been repeating itself the last twenty-four hours ..."

Wentworth paused for a moment, hesitating to speak for a moment, then went on, staring directly into Singh's eyes as he said;

"Let's face it, there's too many rouges out there that over the years have pieced together the connection between myself and the *Spider*. With old weapons returning one after another, who knows what else might return. With Miss Nita here by herself—"

"Say no more, my brother," interrupted the Sikh, his massive frame tightening with resolve, "I have already placed the entire complex in a state of readiness. All alarms are set. All locks in place. I shall guard her with my life, though a thousand devils seek to steal her away, they shall not have her."

Wentworth did not bother to answer, knowing there was no need. Instead, he turned to Jackson, whom he ordered;

"Head down to the garage and pick us out a good heap for the night. I don't know what we might find, if anything, so make it something all purpose. Light armor, good speed. Make sure all its weapons caches are full, and the weapons loaded. And the gas tank is topped off."

Wordlessly, Jackson arose and headed for the garage. Like Singh, the former sergeant was smiling. Ever since December, both men had begun to wonder if their days of finding action at Wentworth's side had come to a close. Neither was so self-absorbed they could wish for a world filled with psychotic murderers and rapine despots. But, if such were to attempt to appear upon the scene, they still wanted to be part of that which barred their entrance.

As the pair moved off to their tasks, Wentworth called out over his shoulder just before he passed through the doorway leading in the direction of the kitchen;

"Oh, and Singh, if you would, tell Jenkyns to unlock the disguise cabinet in my study."

The Sikh nodded, setting out toward the southern wing of the mansion. At the same time, Jackson continued upon his way to the garage. The *Spider* might be forever in retirement, he thought, but at least *something* was going to happen that night, and he thanked his Maker he was going to be a part of it.

9

"GIM'ME another beer, Flora, and can that damn fiddle player before I do somethin' about him meself."

The bar, a fairly nondescript type of place known to the general population as Krenkel's, was a typical corner establishment. It held no kitchen, made no attempt at any particular ambiance. It was simply dedicated to the sale of alcoholic beverages in their many and varied forms—and nothing else.

Krenkel's was also not the kind of place that encouraged much in the way of walk-in patronage, either. Located along the rough and low waterfront section of Manhattan's lower east side, it was situated in a tough, uncompromising neighborhood, a well-known hangout for the worst elements society had to offer. Its patrons were not frolickers looking to have a good time. They were the abused and gray left-overs of society, looking to simply anaesthetize themselves against the coming day.

"Whatever you want, Thump."

The waitress responding to the bruiser at the bar was a plain, tired woman—rumpled, begrudgingly resigned to her sad station in life. Somewhere in her forties, the woman looked quite a bit older. She had not, however, cared about such matters as appearance for some time. The dreams of her youth had all been abandoned in the face of the easiest of the realities laid out before her years earlier. Beaten down young, she had grown into a role which, as it did for so many, ended up fitting her comfortably enough.

"Hey, Jack Benny," she called out in her weary voice. "Cut your strings, will ya? Give it a rest."

In a somewhat clear area in the center of the bar's main room stood the object of the waitress' request, the bent figure of a street violinist—shabbily clothed and pitiful of demeanor. His drooping hat and tattered overcoat were well worn, tired articles. His shoes were scuffed and plain. The man's frazzled gloves were fingerless, so as to allow him to manipulate his bow, something he did with a surprising grace and precision. Despite the opinion of the hulk sitting at the bar nicknamed Thump, the crooked figure playing so soulfully was actually astonishingly well-versed at his craft.

"Hey now, what'dya mean," called out the musician, talking while he continued to play, "why for you'a tella me to stop the playing? I think I playa good."

Obviously not in agreement, Thump slid off his bar stool and turned slowly toward the center of the room, steadying himself against the effect of seven beers as he bellowed;

"I don't care what you think, you little turd. I said I don't want to hear it! Now can the long-haired string boogie or I'll break that damn fiddle over yer head."

The musician pulled his bow across his violin's strings in an exaggeratedly long, but ending fashion, saying;

"Hey, it's okay by me. Whatever you like, good sir. But I tella you now, in alla you life, you never gonna hear no better music than what you hear'a here tonight, played by me, the grrreat Tito Caliepi."

"Yes, Thump. My word ... what's wrong with you? Have you no ear for fine music?"

Most heads in the bar turned toward the direction from which had come the new voice. Thump was the type Flora, as well as most of the tavern's other patrons could easily understand. Big and muscle-bound, slow-witted, easy-to-anger, thick-skulled—he was simply, a common brute. To look at him, one might readily conclude that perhaps he was a dock worker, a high steel builder, or maybe even something unsavory—a thug of some sort.

But whatever he was, any who looked upon him instantly understood he was that direct type of individual who would not hesitate to back any threat without thinking through its possible consequences. It was this simple reason, all concerned were quite certain, which had caused the musician to cease his playing. However, the new player—the man in the corner who questioned Thump, who challenged him—this kind of person they did not understand so readily.

Why, they wondered, would anyone bother to chide a brute like the one at the bar? Where was the profit in it? Where was the sense to it? What, they asked themselves, each and every one, could the fellow possibly hope to gain by such an action? But then, the man hidden in the corner spoke once more, and suddenly all within began to suspect it was not actually Thump with whom the man in the shadows was playing.

"This isn't just any ordinary street bum, some mere penny-kisser, or nickel hustler," continued the man, the tone of his voice taking on a disturbing edge. Chuckling slightly, he added, "You heard him, didn't you? This is none other but the great Tito Caliepi."

Standing, the figure in the shadows proved to be both tall and thin—obviously far too thin a fellow to effectively challenge someone like Thump. But again, for whatever reason he might have in doing so, it was clear to all, including the brute at the bar, that it was the musician with whom this man meant to tangle. Although again, none could see even the slightest reason as to why, all watched him with ghoulish curiosity as he moved away from his table, spreading his hands as he added mockingly;

"The *grrreat* Tito Caliepi."

"Thank'a you, good sir."

Moving out into the open, the thin man brushed back his scraggly brown hair, making an attempt to shove it into place as he continued;

"And I must admit, I've heard your name, Caliepi ..."

"Of'a course you heard my name. Everybody, everywhere ... they all know the *grrreat* master of the violin, Tito Caliepi." Running his bow across his instrument's strings, starting at the top of the neck and moving down to the bridge in a breathless stroke which threw an incredibly sweet note throughout every corner of the tavern, he added;

"Around the world, they'a all know me."

"Oh, it's true. You are so very well known, everywhere—in certain circles, that is, Mr. Caliepi," answered the tall man. Moving forward again, his eyes narrowing sharply, he crossed the room with a slow gait, advancing on the musician, asking as he neared his prey;

"And do you know why this is so?"

"Hey, what'sa matter? What Caliepi do to you?" The bent man pulled in on himself, everything about his body language suggesting he had just suddenly realized he was in trouble. Holding his violin before him protectively, his hands shaking with an increasing nervousness, he stammered;

"Leave'a me alone. I just come in here to play, mak'a the people happy, try to earn a few dollars. A man's gotta eat, you know."

"Oh, indeed yes, Mr. Caliepi, a man does most certainly 'have to eat.' And ... I think we all know how you earn your 'few dollars' whenever you come into an establishment such as this one, don't we?"

Reaching up to his face, scratching casually at his scraggly moustache, wiping his slightly broken nose, the man's face broke into a wide, malevolent grin as he announced;

"The *grrreat* Tito Caliepi is a snitch, everyone. A stool-pigeon. A leaky bag that just can't hold anything inside for very long—not, that is, if there's a handful of pennies to be scooped up."

"He's with the cops," growled Thump accusingly, his entire body suddenly going tense.

"Oh no, no—nothing so ordinary. Mr. Caliepi here is indeed known for prowling the gathering places of rough and ready characters such as yourself and, I'm forced to admit, myself as well, and all our brothers in our bold endeavor, searching for his bits of information. But he does not sell what he finds to anyone as boring as the police, do you, Tito?"

"I don't ..." The musician backed away from the approaching man nervously, his feet seemingly unable to resist tripping over each other. "What, I ... I mean, I don'ta know ... what you'a talking about."

Coming up directly in front of Caliepi, towering over him, his face bathed in the room's dim central light to the point where any could see the small, crescent-shaped scar on his left cheek, the tall man said;

"What I'm talking about is ... why snitch to the police, Caliepi, when instead you can sell what you discover to *the Spider?!*"

Throughout the room, the mention of the believed-to-be-dead crimefighter's name brought a dozen different reactions. Many showed nothing more than simple confusion. Some merely stared at the musician while others began to look back and forth in every direction, suddenly filled with fear. Several rose from their seats, snarling angrily, their voices unleashing pointed threats. Others merely stood and headed immediately for the door. A few leaned forward with sinister curiosity.

But, no reaction to the tall man's accusing words was more surprising than that of Caliepi himself who suddenly straightened. Surprising all by growing more than a half a foot taller with the motion, he took advantage of the distracting moment to bring his bow up and around, slamming it through his accuser's left eye! As the man thrashed and screamed, the musician yanked hard, jerking the ruined orb from its socket and then, in one smooth motion, spinning about and flinging it forward so that it splattered against Thump's face.

"Get the bastard!"

The first to rush Caliepi received a stunning blow as the musician whirled back around and slammed the man across the side of the head with his violin. The instrument shattered, breaking teeth and leaving splinters deep within the cheek of the would-be attacker's face.

"Kill him!"

"You are, all of you," responded Caliepi, standing firm and solid, his voice growing deeper, its accent disappearing, his hands somehow suddenly filling with .45 automatics, "certainly welcome to try."

Without hesitation, the figure no longer pretending to be Tito Caliepi pulled the triggers of both his weapons, sending the closest two of those approaching staggering backward, falling over a table. Of the three men sitting there, only one was able to avoid the falling bodies as their food and drinks were sent crashing to the floor.

"Well," thought Wentworth as he abandoned his street musician disguise completely, "at least I still have a talent for ferreting out these scum, if not for infiltrating them."

Sensing guns other than his own being brought into play, Wentworth threw himself toward the side of the open room, rather than toward its front door, barely avoiding a trio of shots sent his way from multiple directions. Continuing on his course, he hurled himself at the tavern's large, painted-over plate glass window without hesitation. By the time more bullets could be sent after him, he had already fallen below the protecting edge of the window sill. Scrambling quickly, he raced out into the street, knowing Jackson would have certainly heard the shots and already be on his way.

Inside the tavern, however, those within were not about to allow what they believed to be nothing more than a low-grade snitch to make good with his escape. As Wentworth met Jackson and clambered rapidly into the back seat of the coupe they had chosen for that night, men were already pouring into the street after him. Some of them headed for cars of their own, others raced directly into the traffic lanes, pointing their weapons.

Looking into his rear-view mirror, Jackson cursed. Other vehicles were already coming down the one way street behind him, clogging that direction as an avenue of escape. He could not simply throw their car into reverse. With every parking spot filled on both sides, he could not attempt to rush the sidewalk, either. No, their only valid option lay in going forward.

As he crossed his fingers and gunned the accelerator, a wall of lead raced forward to meet him!

10

"DUCK, MAJOR!"

Some fourteen bullets slammed against the coupe's windshield, the overwhelming fusillade hitting with enough force to both crack, then finally shatter the bulletproof glass. Without hesitation, Jackson depressed the car's accelerator until he was mashing it against the floorboard. Swerving as he plowed forward through the crowd of shooters standing in the street, the chauffeur managed to bounce five of them off the vehicle's reinforced grill.

Three of those rammed were thrown sideways, their broken bodies slamming violently against others in the amassed crowd of thugs. The other two ended up falling beneath the coupe's wheels—ribs shattered, bodies crushed.

"Orders," shouted Jackson, to which Wentworth, busy tearing away the bits of make-up with which be had transformed himself into Caliepi, responded;

"Uptown. Brooklyn Bridge. Caliepi speaks with an Italian accent. Most Italians live in Brooklyn. Let's go ahead and mislead them a bit."

Making a wildly sharp turn from Water Street onto Platt, needing to run a red light to do so, Jackson slid smoothly through the coupe's gears, working coolly at building his lead. He had observed a large number of men not only follow his employer from Krenkel's, but duck into cars parked nearby. The chauffeur had no doubts whatsoever that the thugs meant to not only follow the coupe, but to murder whomever they found within it once they had driven it to ground. Feeling he had several excellent reasons to keep such a plan from succeeding, Jackson was in the process of wringing everything he could from the vehicle's engine when Wentworth surprised him by announcing;

"Not quite so fast, Ronald. After all, we wouldn't want to lose such a fine bunch of gentlemen. Not yet, anyway."

"Oh, we wouldn't, would we?" The chauffeur's tone might have been at least slightly joking, but his question was an honest one. Finished removing the last vestiges of Caliepi, Wentworth responded;

"No. I want them to follow us at least far enough to think we actually want to escape to Brooklyn. Misdirection never hurts. On top of that, it's almost certain this bunch is part of the operation we're after. Considering the efficiency they've displayed so far, I think it would be wise to take this opportunity to thin the herd a bit."

"Any ideas on how we're going to accomplish that, major?"

"You handle the wheel work, I'll take care of the rest."

Jackson gave Wentworth a short salute via his rear-view mirror, then turned over his attention completely to his driving. As he did so, despite the fact they were being pursued by at least a score of men all determined to kill them, the chauffeur found himself smiling, feeling positively light-hearted.

"Oh yeah," he thought, his eyes sparkling with anticipation, "I do believe the major's little holiday is damn well looking to be most definitely over."

The lateness of the hour might have ensured clearer streets in almost any other city in the world, but even with the strict gasoline rationing brought about by the war, still Jackson found an incredible amount of traffic in every direction. Watching the way the cars in front of him were moving, the chauffeur spotted a dozen different instances where continuing forward, although the most direct route to their destination, would have resulted in his being forced to stop the coupe completely. Figuring he knew exactly what the outcome of such an action would be, he made his way uptown as best he could, his efforts much more focused on keeping the coupe in constant motion than anything else.

Twice he was forced to double back, heading back downtown, to keep himself and Wentworth from ending up trapped in a sea of hostile cars. Indeed, at one point the chauffeur found himself halfway across Manhattan, closer to its western shore than its eastern one where the Brooklyn Bridge was to be found. After a while, however, even in a city filled with as many reckless drivers as New York, his high speed antics, and those of his pursuers, were finally noticed by the police. As their sirens filled the air, Jackson shouted;

"In case you couldn't tell, we got company, major."

Wentworth took note of the pair of police cars which had fallen in behind the coupe and the half-dozen automobiles pursuing it. Before he could comment, however, gunfire erupted from two of the vehicles following their own. The thugs did not merely fire several rounds in an attempt to discourage the police. Instead they opened fire with what Wentworth believed, from the sound of their fusillade, could only be a trio of machine guns and at least one shotgun.

The first police car went into a wild spin, smashing against several other vehicles before coming to a sickeningly abrupt halt by crashing into a lamp post. The other almost managed to maintain its forward course, then suddenly ran over something unseen which caused it to flip end over end. In its final descent the black and white rammed into two other cars, knocking both of them up onto the sidewalk, all three vehicles tangling with the horrible sounds of twisting metal and the screams of men as they tore through the front of an office building.

"Our friends seem to be playing for keeps," suggested Jackson dryly, ducking as the thugs in the lead pursuit vehicles turned their fire upon the coupe. When Wentworth did not respond, the chauffeur glanced into his rear-view mirror to discover the reason why. Surprisingly, at first he did not see his employer anywhere in sight. Manipulating the mirror, he then spotted Wentworth bent over, working at ripping out the back seat. More than slightly confused, he shouted;

"Boss—what're you doing?"

"I need something from the trunk. And, outside of you stopping so I might hop out to get it, this seems the best course of action."

Jackson did not question his employer further. He had more that enough to occupy his time keeping them ahead of their foes, as well as trying to steer clear of the seemingly never-ending hail of bullets being thrown at them.

"At least," he thought, jamming down the accelerator once more, "we're almost to the bridge."

Jackson mouthed a short, silent prayer over the fact he had not only reached the Brooklyn Bridge on-ramp for which he had been heading, but also that the traffic approaching it was flowing smoothly. Crossing his fingers in the hopes that fact did not change for any reason before they had reached the other side, he swerved once more to put a few additional cars between the coupe and its pursuers.

In the meantime, in the rear of the vehicle, Wentworth had finally managed to remove the back seat, clearing a passage to the trunk. Quickly tearing off the ragged jacket he had been wearing, he shouted;

"I'm going to go through into the trunk. I want you to start letting our friends back there catch up to us. Don't allow them to get alongside us. Just let them position themselves directly behind us."

"Then what?"

"Then, release the trunk lid and keep your head low. I'll take care of the rest."

Jackson sighed, considering all the trouble he had just gone through to put a few cars between the coupe and those following, but said nothing about the matter, however. He trusted Wentworth with his life, had sworn complete and utter devotion to him when they had fought side by side during the Great War.

"You were a soldier then," he reminded himself, "you're a soldier now. And since soldiers follow orders, that, as they say, mister, is that."

The chauffeur heard some slight noises coming from the trunk, but did not put any effort into translating them. He had his assignment, and that job was taking all his concentration. As for knowing which cars were which, he had no trouble identifying their pursuers, even when no one was shooting at him. Jackson had taken care to memorize which cars were after them and, relentless drivers that they were, not one of the six vehicles carrying those out to kill them had failed to keep the coupe in sight.

"Of course," he told himself, "we did have our orders to *let* them keep us in sight. And, speaking of following orders ..."

His eyes locked on the rear-view mirror, hand reaching for the special switch Wentworth had designed and he had installed—the one that would automatically release the trunk lock—Jackson called out even as bullets began to slam around them once more, shouting;

"Okay, they're right on us, major. I'm popping the lid."

And, with a flip of the switch, the coupe's trunk flipped open, allowing Wentworth to stand up in the back of the rapidly moving vehicle, a machine gun in each hand. Taking only the briefest of seconds to make certain of his targets, he fired, sending a score of rounds into each of the two lead cars. In both cases the drivers were slain instantly, the concentration of Wentworth's fire shattering the windshields and shredding both the drivers as well as those in the back seat behind them.

Panic spread through the lead vehicles, but only for an instant. The one which had been in the center lane swerved violently, sliding toward the left hand lane, first crashing into the side of the bridge, them spinning around as two of its tires exploded from the impact. As the shredded rubber smeared across the roadway, the three closest cars behind the ruined one slammed into it as well as to each other. The second pursuit vehicle, which had been coming up in the left hand lane, jerked hard to the left as its dead driver jammed against the steering wheel, nosing into the bridge wall at top speed. Two other cars as well as a truck rammed into it, utterly crushing both it and its occupants.

The result was complete chaos. No cars were able to pass the clogging wreckage. Only two thugs from the pair of vehicles which had somehow avoided the crashed jumble blocking the roadway managed to stumble their way through the twisted, blood-drenched metal to begin opening fire.

They were, however, far too late to be effective.

By the time either of them took their first shot, the coupe had nearly reached the other end of the bridge. And although Wentworth had not ducked, had made no attempt to return to the relative safety of the back seat, and instead had remained standing, taunting his enemies with his presence, Jackson had moved the coupe well out of range of anything but the luckiest shot.

Indeed, the thugs were at such a distance they could not even make out for certain whether or not Wentworth was still standing up within the trunk. They could, however, hear a faint trace of a flat and mocking laughter, a sound that terrified the both of them for some reason neither could understand.

11

RAM SINGH, tray in hand, the great hound Apollo sitting patiently at his bare feet, stood outside of Wentworth's study for several long minutes, debating which course of action might be the best one for him to take next. He had met with both Wentworth and Jackson when they had returned to Sutton Place, helping them get the greatly damaged coupe into the back of the complex's underground garage unseen. Its windows cracked and shattered, much of its paint job marred by gunfire, it would need a massive amount of work before it could once again be used in public without drawing far too much unneeded attention toward its owner.

As they had done so, Jackson had made quite a great commotion, enthusiastically relating the quite spectacular manner in which Wentworth had dealt with the thugs who had pursued them. When he reached the part in the story where the criminologist had risen up out of the trunk to strike down their foes, the chauffeur commented on how terrific it made him feel to finally have the *Spider* returned to the world and back in action. His smile wide, he had shouted;

"After all this time, major, wow—all I'm saying is, just what I thought then, I am just damn happy to see your little holiday is finally over."

Wentworth had turned to his one-time sergeant then, his face calm, his eyes looking almost sad. In a voice edged with anger, but calmed with the tone of a teacher trying to get through to an unruly class, he said;

"Try to understand this, please ... my putting aside of certain aspects of my life has not been merely some 'little holiday,' Ronald. And, as for the path I have chosen to now walk, I have not come to the end of it. It is by no means over. The force we knew as the *Spider* is dead. And he's going to stay that way."

"But ... it's just ... I mean—"

"I understand your feelings," Wentworth said quietly, "and in many ways, I can sympathize. But, you must accept the simple truth that ... that period of my life had been completed." Realizing his statement might seem to be contradicted by his actions earlier that night, he added;

"As for the past couple of days, I am helping Kirkpatrick with this case because I feel more than a little responsible for what is happening in our city these past few days. As the *Spider*, I was reckless—overly confident. And, it is that confidence which ultimately made me sloppy in my work. I should have been more thorough, should have made certain devices like the Green Fire never again fell into criminal hands." Staring at Jackson, unblinking, his eyes suddenly as stern as the chauffeur had ever seen them, Wentworth added;

"I went undercover tonight the way any duly appointed officer of the law might. Finding the man with the crescent-shaped scar on his cheek after trying only four such establishments was a rare bit of luck, and one that, having now met this fellow close up, has proved that this is indeed a case worth looking into." When Jackson and Singh merely stood waiting for their employer to explain, Wentworth had continued, telling them;

"These people, whatever they're up to, whomever they are, they've done their homework. I will admit to you freely, I was quite taken aback when that fellow recognized the name 'Tito Caliepi.' The fact that he believed Caliepi to be a snitch working for the *Spider* tells me this bunch knows how to read between the lines, how to analyze data and draw intelligent conclusions." The criminologist spoke for another handful of seconds on the subject, then finally concluded, saying;

"For our own good, and that of the city, these villains must be stopped. And they will be ... but not by the *Spider*."

But not by the Spider.

The words echoed bitterly within Singh's mind. For the past few months the massive Sikh had waited patiently for Wentworth to tire of his new pose. Any man, Singh was willing to admit, deserved to take a rest from his labors on occasion. And, for more than ten years Wentworth had struggled with a Herculean effort against unimaginable odds. He had battled entire armies almost single-handedly. He had been stabbed and shot, bludgeoned and electrocuted. His enemies had come in both sexes, all sizes, and in seemingly never-ending waves.

Singh had first met Wentworth in India, close to twenty years previous. The one the Sikh thought of then as "unworthy," "unclean," came into his life on a wave of thunder, saving both Singh and his father from certain death. At that point, as a matter of honor, he had followed the traditions of his caste and creed, pledging himself to he who had acted as savior for his chieftain father as well as himself. His opinion of Wentworth did not change immediately, however.

But not by the Spider.

At first, his going off with and working alongside the upstart intruder to his native land had been a thing of obligation only. He had, in fact, quite seriously planned to merely bide his time, to await the moment when Wentworth's "true" nature would reveal itself—when the outsider would finally prove through his actions that his claimed intentions were false.

Then, the Sikh had told himself smugly, he would strike the pretender down and be done with him.

But, that day had never come.

As days and weeks had turned into months and years, never once did the intruder disappoint. Never did he do an unworthy thing, back a dishonorable cause, misuse his power, seek the adoration of the crowd. Indeed, if anything, he had denied himself all comfort, all pleasures. He had put aside the pleasures most men took for granted, and dedicated himself to fanning the flames of justice in a world gone chill with evil.

Of course, as Richard Wentworth he was obliged to

play a certain part in a particular manner. He needed to be seen drinking and socializing, laughing at the correct times with the right people. But, ultimately it was all nothing more than a mask which had to be worn—

"No," Singh thought, "not worn ... *endured*."

In their first years together, the *Spider* had not yet existed, but still had the two fought back the ever-encroaching tides of darkness at every opportunity. They had thrown themselves into a vast variety of dangers, against all manner of monsters, and they had earned their places in the Heaven to come a thousand times over.

And, when such battles had become too complicated for them to wage, when they found themselves confronted by too many outside forces to be able to act effectively, then had Wentworth sought a new face to put before the world. Considering that he had already been marking the foreheads of those he had slain with his vermilion seal for some time, branding them with the outline of an ugly spider, he decided then that was what he would become.

But not by the Spider.

And become such he had, with a swift and terrible vengeance. The *Spider*, the Master of Men, savior of no one knew how many millions, had become a human weapon unparalleled.

"But, no blade can be used forever. Even the mightiest sword must be honed again and again to keep its edge." Peeking inside Wentworth's study, catching just the barest glimpse of the man he was honored to call "Sahib," he thought;

"For as it is said, how many times can the same steel be sharpened before it has been ground down too far? How much can a warrior ask of any one weapon?"

Wentworth, he knew, had not abandoned their mission. As he had changed the way they would go about accomplishing it in the past, so now he was doing so again. Thinking back to his days in India, he remembered that his father had also not led their people in a rigid manner. Despite the fact tradition called for many things to be done over and over in the same manner, his father had more than once defied the old ways.

As he stared at Wentworth, the great Sikh remembered an occasion upon which his father had taken him aside, and with a twinkle in his eye, had explained;

"Rules created in an age of scimitars and goat carts may perhaps sometimes need a bit of revision in a time of cannons and airplanes."

Opening the door wide, Singh motioned to Apollo to enter the room. The old dog walked straight to Wentworth, sitting down next to his master's chair in the exact spot where his head would be most conveniently positioned for Wentworth to reach over and scratch it. As always, the dog was rewarded for his precision, Wentworth digging his nails into Apollo's scalp, and around his ears, exactly the way the dog enjoyed it most.

"So," asked Wentworth as he continued to shower the Great Dane with affection, "what brings you two here in the middle of the night? Finally decide you've had enough of my 'little holiday,' as Jackson calls it? Ready to head back to India now that the *Spider* is no more?"

"I have been told by yourself and many of your society associates that I make the best cocktails in the city," replied Singh. "When I go the market, I have an unerring eye for choosing the freshest vegetables. For the amusement of children, I have been known to perform magic tricks. True things, yes?" When Wentworth nodded in agreement, the

Sikh continued, saying;

"Bartender or lackey? Master shopper or housewife? Magician or entertainer of children? We all wear many masks so that we do not tire of the terrible visage which is our true face."

Moving forward, Singh placed the tray containing a small cup and a pot of strong tea he had brought for Wentworth on the square of ceramic tile kept on his desk for just such purposes. Looking directly into Wentworth's eyes, the massive Sikh said;

"We have marched into Hell side by side for longer than we have done anything else. Someday we will finally reach its final gates, and when we do we will confront the Devil himself, and it shall be a bloody and wonderful struggle of most glorious proportions. When that day comes, does it matter which face we show him, as long as we do so while spilling his demon blood across the floor of eternity?"

"No," answered Wentworth, much brightened by his long-time companion's response. "Not in the least."

Ram Singh made a short bow, then turned and left the room. Putting aside the pen he had been using, still absently scratching Apollo's head, Wentworth reached for the tea pot. Pouring himself a cupful, he thought;

"It's better this way. It's time to bring a little balance into my life—all our lives. Justice will still be served, the wicked will still be punished. It just won't be in such a colorful fashion anymore."

Sipping at his tea, Wentworth smiled. He would never go so far as to call Singh a housewife, but he had to admit the Sikh knew his way around a kitchen far better than he himself did.

"Better than Nita, too," he said aloud, his tone one using a joke to cover the truth, "eh, Apollo?"

The Great Dane responded with a short bark, pulling a small chuckle from within his master. Grateful, he scratched the dog's head and neck for another minute, then finally made the ending pass with his hand down over the bridge of Apollo's nose which signified that their moment was finished. Superbly trained, the large hound walked over to his favorite area rug within the study and, after making several circles, curled up upon it and closed his eyes.

Wentworth watched the dog for a moment, then returned to his work. He had been drawing up a list of things he wanted to go over with Kirkpatrick the next day. He would have to meet with the commissioner early, since some official function or another was going to command his time during the afternoon.

Still, having run across the man with the crescent-shaped scar, he wanted to follow up on that thread. And, having the resources of the New York City police department at his disposal would actually make such a search easier by far.

"One of those things," he said quietly, "that is certainly easier for criminologist Richard Wentworth than it is for the *Spider*."

And, with that thought uttered, Wentworth congratulated himself one last time on the decision to put his alter-ego to bed once and for all. For a while he had debated the wisdom in doing so, but now he was certain. It had been a good idea. An intelligent one. One with which, he admitted to himself, he was quite happy.

He would remain happy with the idea for only another thirteen hours.

12

"WELL," said Wentworth, finally finished reviewing the sheaf of papers in his hand, "that, as they say, is that."

The criminologist was commenting on what would be the first report delivered to the commissioner's office from the medical examiner's department. Bodies from the airborne attack which had taken place the day before had already been studied extensively, in fact, were still being studied even as the criminologist and Kirkpatrick were meeting.

That initial report produced, however, was all the two men needed at that time. It had come to the same conclusion both Wentworth and Kirkpatrick had made the previous afternoon as they had stared through the plate glass window of Rosanti's. Although it never hurt when spinning theories to have solid facts for confirmation, neither of them had actually needed any form of science to identify the horror they had been witnessing. Just like the Green Fire the night before, another of the terrible murder machines of the past they knew all too intimately was reaching forward in time once more.

"Yes, on the surface, at least."

Twice before criminals bent on blackmailing their way to riches had poisoned many of the city's staple products. After the second occurrence, police scientists had concluded that those behind the new attack had indeed built upon the work of those who had tried such means first. The assault of the day before had now been scientifically proved to definitely be a further refinement of the same process.

"What do you mean, Stanley?"

Kirkpatrick sat behind his desk, fingers bridged before his face, eyes unfocused. Clearing his throat, he allowed his hands to separate so that he might use them to loosen his tie slightly. Afterward, he lowered them until their palms were touching his blotter, then said;

"The robbery at the train the other night ... seemed straight-forward enough. Murder everyone, rob them, leave no witnesses. Just as it happened ten years ago. String us along, make us think it was merely an old trick being brought back. You saw through that much, though—"

"Well, I ..."

"Please, Richard, don't disappoint me by falling into false modesty. You were right. That whole sordid business with those poor girls ... the delivery of the photos to the *Bugle*—"

"Pardon me," interrupted Wentworth, "but tell me, what do you think of that, of this bunch sending their photos to the *Bugle*? Any thoughts on why them?"

"To be honest," answered Kirkpatrick in a straight-forward voice, "because I believe they looked at the papers in the city with the biggest circulation and decided to go with the most disreputable one. Martin Basilton still has something of a reputation, but he leaves too much of the day to day to that cigar-chewing slug of his, Stanton. I don't believe this gang would have had to study the intricacies of New York City journalism for very long to choose Stanton as the editor who would do their dirty work for them."

Wentworth nodded in sad agreement. Apologizing once more for his interruption, he asked Kirkpatrick to continue with his original thought. Without hesitation, the commissioner jumped back saying;

"My belief is that what happened at the train, as you

deduced, was no mere robbery at all. Just the set-up for yesterday."

"And what are your thoughts on yesterday?"

Wentworth studied his old friend, waiting for his answer. He had been laboring over what connection there might be between the two crimes himself, and was curious to see what Kirkpatrick had made of the situation.

"That's the problem. I'm not entirely certain. Yesterday's attack should have ultimately been followed by some sort of ransom demand. You would think. That's what was done the first few times. And, I mean, what's the point of such murders otherwise? Not like the Green Fire where you can rob the victims at your leisure. But so far, no demands. Not to us, the mayor's office, Albany. Nothing."

"Not at all straight-forward."

"Hell," cursed the commissioner. "Nothing these jackals have done has been straight-forward."

"I have to admit, I agree." Turning his head sideways, his mouth a grim line, Wentworth said, "We're being led somewhere. There's no doubt they're working quite hard to keep us off our game, like those Indian tribes that would stampede herds of buffalo, driving them toward a cliff edge. No hard work killing their prey. Just chase them until they fall and pick up the pieces afterward."

Both men went silent for a moment. Each in their own way was essentially a man of action. Each appreciated the advantages to be found in studying a crime and its components, of course, before simply rushing bullheaded into a situation. But, with monsters loose, preying on the citizens of their city, they could not help but to feel a certain anxiety over not seeing any way to prepare for what might be coming next. Hoping to be able to uncover some small insight, Wentworth asked;

"By the way, did you manage to get the reports on that situation at the Brooklyn Bridge last night?"

Digging through the folders stacked in the "incoming" box on his desk, the commissioner pulled out the one Wentworth had asked for, handing it over to his friend. As the criminologist opened it and began reading, Kirkpatrick asked;

"What's your thought?"

"I don't know," answered Wentworth in a distracted voice. Not wishing to tell the commissioner the truth, that he was certain he had tangled with young Jerry's man with a crescent-shaped scar, he offered instead;

"Read about it in the morning edition. Machine guns used to murder police men. Wrecked cars on the Brooklyn Bridge, plenty of blood and bodies ..."

"There're more criminals in New York than just this new bunch, you know."

"I realize that, but I just wondered if we might not be able to draw any lines from one thing to another."

What Wentworth was actually doing was searching the report to see if either Thump, or the man he had come to think of in his head as simply "Scar," had shown up in the morgue. If they were among the dead, then that quite promising lead would have been closed to him.

Not finding anyone even close to their description listed there, however, cheered Wentworth considerably. Finishing the report, happy to discover that Thump and Scar were still out in the city—somewhere where he might be able to find them once more—the criminologist said;

"So, what next, Stanley?"

"We're running ballistics checks on the bullets recovered from last night—from the bridge and a place called Krenkel's."

"Yes," mused Wentworth absently, not betraying his involvement with the goings on in the tavern, "the bar mentioned in the article. They seemed to think whatever occurred last night started there."

"That's right," said Kirkpatrick. His tone low, he added, "you know who else was there?"

Putting down the papers in his hand, looking up as innocently as he could, Wentworth shrugged slightly, asking;

"No, who?"

"Tito Caliepi."

"The vagabond violinist? Really? I thought he was dead. What was he doing there?"

The commissioner eyed his friendly coldly for a long moment. Back before he had seen the *Spider* slain by Wentworth, back when he had often times suspected his friend of actually being the elusive criminal, he had often wondered if he might not use the mask of Caliepi as well. Wentworth was, after all, a violinist of great renown. The commissioner stared for a long moment, then finally dismissed his notion, saying instead;

"Don't know, really. Witnesses that would talk say that the fight broke out over his playing. Have an APB out for him, just for questioning."

"Couldn't hurt," offered Wentworth in an off-handed manner. Turning back to the papers he had set down, he asked what else was being done about the incident of the previous evening. Looking out the window, wondering what might be headed toward his city next, Kirkpatrick offered;

"We're working on identifying those bodies we don't know yet. Looking into known associates of those we did identify. Don't know if that bunch has anything to do with our new friends or not, but the boys are pretty hot about it.

After all, cop killers aren't something that gets tolerated by any police force."

Kirkpatrick went silent for a moment, then snapped his fingers, asking;

"You know, what if last night was another set-up? Just as we were purposely set up by the careful arrangement of school girls, what if this is another distraction?"

Wentworth knew, of course, that the notion was not a valid one, but had no way to prove such an opinion without revealing his part in the previous evening's events. His lack of enthusiasm for the idea was enough to put Kirkpatrick onto other theories he had dreamed up over the night. The two went around in circles over what few facts they did have, arguing, theorizing for a little more than another hour, when the commissioner took note of the time as shown on his desk clock. His hands moving to pull his tie taunt once more, he said;

"This will have to do it for now." When Wentworth questioned why they needed to stop working, Kirkpatrick explained;

"There's nothing stopping you, but I've got one of those annoying civic duties to perform." Suddenly snapping his fingers, Wentworth said;

"Wait, that's right, you're receiving that lifetime achievement award from the Ladies Auxiliary today. How could I forget? Nita's one of the speakers."

"I'll tell you how you forgot," answered Kirkpatrick, chuckling as he did so, "it's because these kinds of affairs are deadly dull. Rubber chicken luncheon, hours of speeches and polite applauds. I don't know how you avoided having to accompany Nita, but you're a lucky man."

"Well, it's true," admitted Wentworth, smiling at his friend's obvious discomfort, thinking once more of the woman he loved. "I am a lucky man. But, I'll tell you what. Just so you'll have something positive to think about, picture this. While you're chewing away at your galvanized rooster, I'll be sitting at my usual table at the Cobalt Club—a nice tumbler of Scotch in hand, enjoying a rare sirloin. Baby potatoes, glazed carrots."

"Oh God, but you're a heartless bastard," joked the commissioner. Then, glancing at his desk calendar, realizing what day of the week it was, his voice took on a darker tone as he added;

"Wait, isn't today the day William bakes, makes those nugget rolls, with the butter glazing, and the sesame seeds?" When Wentworth just smiled in response, Kirkpatrick sighed mightily, asking;

"You wouldn't like to trade places, would you? I mean, you could use another award—couldn't you?"

The two traded quips for a moment longer, then rose from their chairs. The commissioner had to be on time for his ceremony, and Wentworth had an appointment in the police's central photo storage facility. He had volunteered to go through the thousands of available mug shots in the hopes of finding one that matched the description Jerry the newsboy had given them.

Of course, the task did not seem nearly as daunting to Wentworth as it did his friend. The criminologist had, after all, actually met the man with the crescent-shaped scar the night before. He knew exactly what the man looked like. If, however, he could find Scar's photo, he would then also have uncovered the man's complete history as well—last known address, legal name, aliases, et cetera.

Kirkpatrick also did not know that Wentworth had Jackson and Singh calling all the hospitals in the area in the hopes of finding one where a man was treated for having one of his eyes pulled from his head. The criminologist had an unshakable feeling that Scar was deeply involved with the new gang they were hunting, and was determined to find him at any cost.

As the pair left Kirkpatrick's office, a certain inner peace had begun to descend over Wentworth. As daunting as the task of stopping the monsters who had so recently descended on their city had seemed only the day before, suddenly pieces were beginning to come together for him.

As they always did.

Saying "goodbye" to the commissioner on the second floor, Wentworth headed for the file room while Kirkpatrick continued down the stairs for the front door. By the time Wentworth had reached the room he needed, he was surprised to find his spirits so buoyed he was actually whistling.

He would remain in such a mood for only another hour and forty-four minutes. After which, it was quite possible, he would never know happiness again.

13

"WILL THERE be anything else, sir?"

"No, actually. Thank you, officer, but I do believe what I have here in this envelope will be more than enough to make the commissioner the happiest man in New York City."

The supervising sergeant on duty in the records department commented as he gave Richard Wentworth a snappy salute that, if the criminologist could actually make Stanley Kirkpatrick a happy man, then he was welcome at headquarters anytime. Several of the other officers rendered pleasant greetings to him as well as he left the building.

There was nothing false in their doing so.

Wentworth was well respected for his ability to understand the criminal mind and to predict the actions of such persons. This held true not only in New York City, or on the American eastern seaboard, but across the country, and even in many locales overseas. The criminologist held high ranking positions on investigatory panels and commissions in a half-dozen countries. His papers on crime, on its causes and effects, its prevention, early discouragement, and the such, were widely respected. They were also often highly criticized.

Despite the extreme regard in which he was held as a progressive thinker, Wentworth was difficult for many of his fellow experts to classify. He believed in societal responsibility, in rehabilitation and making an effort to not merely punish, but to understand the wrong-doer as well. In this respect he reflected the deeply cherished feelings of many of his peers, especially those who rarely traveled outside the circles of academia.

However, where he differed dramatically from the majority of his fellows was in his firm stance that understanding the law-breaker was one thing, but pampering them was quite another. Wentworth believed in harsh punishment for wrong-doers, and had little use for the never-ending, endless mercy espoused by the "bleeding hearts" to be found within his discipline.

He also felt that law-makers should not, as he put it, "attempt to legislate morality." A man stealing a loaf of bread to feed his family during a Depression was not motivated by the same instincts as one who stole the same loaf to sell to someone else. His constant call for an intelligent, educated judiciary, and not one made up of political cronies, made him few friends as well.

But, it was these attitudes which did sit well with either party bosses or the intelligentsia which made him so popular with the cops in the street. Those who actually worked in law-enforcement, and did not merely theorize about it, both sought out and enjoyed his company. They knew all too well there were reasons for criminal behavior—broken homes, alcoholic parents, the miserable environments to be found within so many of the ghettos which existed in the world's major cities. Those officers who actually patrolled the city's dark avenues, they walked the streets and saw the sad and miserable circumstances which shaped criminal minds every day.

But, what the local beat cop understood, and most academics did not, was that just as the most depraved murderers and miserable thieves came from such backgrounds, so to did doctors and lawyers, caring clergymen, giving teachers, as well as highly decorated service men and a thousand other types of productive citizens the world needed desperately. Yes, any policeman would admit, where one grew up and how they were raised did certainly play a part in any person's development. But, they also knew such factors were not more important than the basic make-up of the person themselves.

"There's no such thing as a bad boy."

As he walked out into the crisp afternoon sunlight, Wentworth shuddered as he once more heard within his mind the hackneyed cliché which so many of his contemporaries believed with an unshakable faith. Stopping for just a moment, he opened the envelope he was carrying and pulled forth the photos it contained, if for no other reason that to present himself with all the proof he might need that he was not wrong in his beliefs.

"Thump," a.k.a. Robert Johnson, and the fellow

Wentworth had named "Scar," whose given name was "Brian Carnahan," these were not of a sort who might have turned out any differently if they had been born into high society. They were thoroughly, completely evil men, and had been their entire lives.

Having a name for the larger of the two, Wentworth had found Johnson easily enough by checking "known aliases." After he had uncovered "Thump" within the department's records, he had then searched through Johnson's "known acquaintances" until he had discovered Carnahan. Each man had a rap sheet running several pages. Both had started their separate lives of crime before they had reached the age of ten.

"There might not be any bad boys in this world," thought the criminologist wearily, "but there certainly are some rotten ones."

Continuing on his way, Wentworth found Jackson parked and waiting for him in one of the spots reserved for official police business. As he both checked his mirrors and started his engine, the chauffeur reported that so far his and Singh's search for a man having been treated for eye trauma had turned up nothing in the way of results. The criminologist sighed as he climbed into the back seat of his limousine, responding that he had not actually thought it would.

"This group is well organized," Wentworth explained with a slight grunt of resignation. "Knowing they have their own dark room and photographer, I had little doubt they would possess their own doctor as well."

"So, where to, Major?"

Wentworth directed Jackson to head uptown, specifically to the assembly hall where the commissioner was to receive his honor that afternoon. He wanted to share his discovery of the man with the crescent-shaped scar's identity, if not the true reason as to why he was so certain he had uncovered the correct scarred cheek. Also, and perhaps more importantly to Wentworth, Nita would be there.

Nita.

His Nita. The woman he loved. The woman who made all his struggles worthwhile. For years he had believed he battled the injustice which flooded the world only because it had to be done by those who could. He was no adventurer, an empty heart out to capture glory. He was not a bored playboy, a lost soul looking to shape a more meaningful existence for himself. Nor was he driven by demons of guilt.

He had become the *Spider* because mankind needed such an individual, and he was one of the few men ever born who could fill such a role. Since the beginning, he did what he did simply because it *had* to be done by someone. But, realizing that a need exists, and having the fortitude to do something about it had proved to be two different things.

Wentworth had realized years earlier that he could not have gone on as long as he had without Nita by his side. Arguing with her kept his mind sharp, his mission clearly defined within his brain. She inspired him. Rather, unlike those females who loved out of a need to see themselves completed by another, she did not attempt to hold him back, to "keep him safe." Instead, more often than not, she was the bow which launched him straight and true at one target after another.

When he had killed the false *Spider* months earlier, he had been thinking of Nita, of what it would mean to her if it had actually been himself that had been dispatched. He knew she would not dissolve into the copious tears expected by society. His respect for her was too great that he would insult her thus. She was the woman who, after all, when he himself had been incapacitated, had donned the make-up and costume of the *Spider* and gone out into the night herself—guns in hand, righteous fire within her heart.

When the false *Spider* had lain dead before him, Wentworth had realized Fate was handing him a golden opportunity. Let the *Spider* die, a voice from the back of his mind had whispered to him. You have served long enough—let this cup pass.

In an instant, his brain laid out a possible future for him. With the *Spider* officially dead, he could still fight crime, still wage war against the endless forces of evil, but he could cease to be a target himself while doing so. A man in his twenties believes himself capable of changing the world. A man forty years old, however, begins to find the ambitions of youth often somewhat out of reach.

Exhausted, weary, he had posed himself a challenge. Let the official verdict of the *Spider*'s death stand for at least a few months. Wait until your fortieth birthday. Then, after that brief handful of weeks rest, then make your decision.

And, accepting the challenge, he had rested and healed, and day by day had looked at the world around him. His city was still just as torn by crime as it had been before he had first raised his hand against its wickedness and corruption. He had made his pledge to turn the tide because of the horrors he had struggled against during the Great War. And, after two decades of being able to do no more than hold the line against such things, he now lived in a world immersed in an even greater conflict than the one which had affected him so.

"No," he had told himself, "our time is done. Let someone else take over. Maybe the next man will do a better job. Considering the state of things in the world even after all my efforts ... well, perhaps I just wasn't good enough."

Over the years he had proposed to Nita more than once. She had always accepted. They had rented halls, booked churches, hired musicians, sent out invitations—more times than he wished to remember. But, somehow, something had always interfered. Something had always stood in their way. Something that demanded the attention of the *Spider*.

"Well," he said softly in the back seat of his limousine, "no more."

Days earlier at his birthday party, at the moment when Kirkpatrick had come up and taken him off to investigate the return of the Green Fire, he had been just about to propose once more. As events had unfolded in the gelid March night outside the Bronx, a terrible cold had slithered through his body, a hideous notion that chewed at his nerves. It whispered that he did not deserve happiness, that no matter what he did, something—*something*—would always be there to make certain he never achieved it. Walking into the fourth Pullman car, seeing the terrible display made of the young women targeted and used by the new cabal of brutes Destiny had arranged against him, he had for a moment accepted what lie before him as his responsibility.

And then, he had cast the notion aside.

No, he declared emphatically, he was *not* responsible for the wickedness of other men. He was not his brother's keeper. Not any longer. From that moment forward, he told himself, he would do what was required of decent human beings, but no more.

Before he had been taken to the lonely section of train tracks outside the city, he had been seconds away from asking Nita to be his. Once again, he realized on his way home, events had cascaded around him conspiring to steal from out his grasp any chance of happiness he might have.

He had told himself the day before that he would do

his duty and then get on with his own life, only to have the sky darken and the streets fill with death. Once more he had gone out and done more than any other man would do, because of duty. Because of honor.

"Almost there, Major."

As the grand auditorium came into view, Wentworth pushed all his warring thoughts from his head. He had done all he planned to do. He would give Kirkpatrick what he had discovered as soon as the luncheon had concluded, and then, then he would do what *he* wanted for once.

The second he found Nita, the moment they were together, he told himself, he would propose. He would tell Jackson to give him the keys to the limousine and to take the subway home. He would then escort his beloved to the passenger side door, see her safely inside, and then the two of them would leave the city, drive to Connecticut, find a small town with a bed and breakfast and simply not return to New York until they were man and wife.

"I'm coming, sweetheart."

Sitting alone, staring out through the windshield at the approaching auditorium, Richard Wentworth smiled. His mind was clear. His resolve firm. For one brief moment, he could see his entire future laid out before him.

And then, his time ran out, and the city block before him disappeared in a thundering explosion that blotted out the sky!

14

"NITA!"

Wentworth threw himself from his limousine and raced forward into the oncoming fury. When the explosion had erupted, the monstrous force of it had stopped traffic instantaneously, the staggering size of the detonation practically beyond belief. Stone, steel and glass had been hurled upward and outward with incredible volatility, the tons of shrapnel created slaughtering hundreds in the streets. Hundreds more in the affected buildings. And, all around the roadways themselves crumbled, concrete and asphalt shattered for a quarter mile in every direction.

"Nita!"

Wentworth made his way forward as best he could through the overwhelming madness. Those pedestrians in the area still able to stand were all stumbling blind, groping their way through the massive, mounting clouds of dust and dirt billowing wildly through the avenues. The bodies of the dead and dying were strewn everywhere, broken and torn, whole and in pieces. None of the living could hear anything, due to the deafening force of the explosion. Which actually was for the best, for there was nothing to be heard there in the choking nightmare except the terrible screams of the injured and the dying.

"Nita!"

Most of the cars on the block had been badly damaged, if not completely crushed by flying debris. The only thing that had saved Wentworth and Jackson the fate of so many others was the fact all the cars in the criminologist's small fleet were specially made, their windows bulletproof, their roofs and bodies filled with reinforcing bars and struts. Jackson had unfortunately been thrown against the steering wheel, his forehead torn open. Safer in the well-padded back seat, Wentworth had escaped any kind of major injury, but was now risking far worse than his chauffeur had received by daring to run through the streets.

Choking on the gray and swirling air, thick as it was with

detritus, Wentworth pulled out his handkerchief and held it over his mouth and nose. The momentary hesitation to catch his breath saved the criminologist's life for, only seconds after he paused, the street before him erupted as a spark reached one of the ruptured gas lines running underneath the sidewalk. The devastating explosion was quickly followed by a massive fireball, a terrifying display which blazed forth from under the ruined avenue, igniting great sections of the floating debris, filling the air around everyone with flame.

Spared being directly within the center of the eruption due to his delay, still was Wentworth too close to the blast. Thrown violently from his feet, his hands and face singed, he landed badly on the broken sidewalk, his back colliding with a sharp, upturned slab of cracked cement. Trying to stand, his hands groped for something with which he might pull himself erect, but they could find nothing.

Then, before Wentworth could assemble his thoughts, a second, and then a third, underground explosion followed the first as additional gas mains ruptured. The criminologist was hurled upward into the air, landing badly once more against the shattered street below. His head cracking sharply against a bent and wobbling parking meter, Wentworth did his best to stand, but discovered he could not. His legs refusing to follow his commands, they folded beneath him, dropping him face first into the street where he remained, with the rest of the multiple explosion's victims, his mind shutting down as he thought despairingly—

"Nita ..."

"NITA...?"

Wentworth awoke to darkness. After mumbling his beloved's name, he forced himself to remain quiet as his brain swam back to consciousness, hoping to be able to identify where he was by sounds alone. As the fog swirling through his mind began to lift, he realized not only from the noises he could make out, but certain of the smells which he could discern as well, that he must be in a hospital. He also quickly discovered that he had not gone blind, nor been placed within darkness.

"Major," Jackson's voice sounded. "Was that you? Did you speak?"

"Yes ..." a part of Wentworth's brain was stunned at how terrible he sounded. Scraping at his face awkwardly, his fingers not quite responding to the directions being sent to them by his mind, Wentworth still managed to remove the damp cloth which had been placed over his eyes. Blinking hard, he asked;

"W-Where...?"

"St. Christopher's. It was the closest hospital to the side of the explosion you were on."

"The ... the side I was on?" Wentworth stared at Jackson, confusion filling his eyes. Still somewhat groggy, not quite able to understand the chauffeur's meaning, he asked;

"What do you ... what are you saying?"

"The explosion, major, it was huge. Gigantic. Took out the entire assembly hall, the entire block—more." Jackson looked over his shoulder, making certain no one else was within earshot, then added;

"Considering what's been going on, I think it might be another bit of the past coming back to haunt us."

Wentworth's mind raced for only a moment, stumbling over the pain and weariness still coursing through his body—and then he remembered. It had been years earlier, yet another gang of blackmailers, but this time armed with an incredibly powerful explosive, an insane compound so volatile that, if that were indeed what had been used that day, a lump no larger than a small grape would have been all that was needed to create the devastation through which he had somehow lived. And then, his eyes went wide, his heartbeat stopping within his chest as he shouted;

"Nita?"

As Wentworth surged forward, throwing a monumental effort into lifting his head from his pillow, he shouted in sudden pain even as Jackson moved forward, looking to hold his employer down, telling him;

"She's alive. She's alive. Calm down. You're going to hurt yourself. Lie down. Please, lie down. She's alive."

His jaw vibrating, eyes staring, mouth hanging open, Wentworth gasped against the agony which had filled his body when he thrust himself forward, then allowed himself to be eased back onto his bed. Jackson sighed with relief, realizing the criminologist had come within inches of jerking loose the various tubes needled into his arm.

How Wentworth was even capable of movement, the chauffeur was not sure. His face had been covered with an ointment-drenched cloth because of the burns he had received. His back and left side, left arm and leg, were covered with bruises and gashes. The doctor assigned to him reported that he had lost a massive amount of blood. Amazingly, nothing had been broken. But he had been savagely abused by the series of gas main explosions. Indeed, the doctor had assured Jackson that, considering the dose of sedatives he had been given, his employer would probably not awaken until late the next day.

But, only three hours after seeing the world fly apart from the back seat of his limousine, Richard Wentworth was awake. His mind was swirling, confused and dulled by the effects of massive blood loss, as well as the drugs he had received. But, he thought, as he allowed his head to sag limply back into his pillow, it mattered not. He would endure.

Nita was alive.

Somehow she had lived through the terrible explosion he had seen. It was a miracle. Nothing less than Divine intervention could have allowed her to survive. But, survive she had. He knew it. Jackson had told him so.

"But," a voice from the darker region of his mind whispered, the section ruled by suspicion, "if she's alive, then where is she? Why isn't she here?"

Steeling himself, a dread creeping through his brain and heart and soul colder than he had ever known, Wentworth summoned all his remaining strength so as to be able to control himself. Then, certain that he would cause himself no further injury, he focused his attention on Jackson, and asked;

"Nita. If she's alive ... where is she?"

At first the chauffeur could not look Wentworth directly in the eye. When his employer's cracked and blistered hand caught hold of his sleeve and began to pull, Jackson finally lifted his head and said quietly;

"I said she was alive, major, and she is. But ... c'mon, she was inside the assembly hall when it went up. She got, ummm, pretty banged up."

His fingers encircling Jackson's wrist, Wentworth squeezed the chauffeur's arm, his words hissing between his clenched teeth as he demanded;

"You will explain to me ... in exacting detail ... the phrase ... 'banged up.'"

"Okay, okay, sure. She's hurt bad. But, c'mon, what would you expect, major? Broken bones. Both her legs, I think. Arm and shoulder, they said. Bunch of ribs ... ahhhh ... I mean, she lost a lotta blood, like you, and ... what else?"

"What else?"

Wentworth's body began to shake, arms and legs vibrating, head throbbing. *If you had only done as you wished,* a voice within his mind mocked him, *you would have already been gone. Away from this nightmare. But no, not you. Kirkpatrick taps your shoulder and your life is put on hold—again.*

"What *else?*"

"She's got some, something wrong ... internal ..."

Lurching awkwardly, fumbling within his bed, Wentworth sat up, not waiting to hear any more. Resisting the overwhelming urge to collapse, he steeled himself against the new onrush of pain, pushed aside his body's insistence he surrender to his injuries. Ripping the tubes from his arm, he cast them aside, not noticing that one of the three needles taped to his arm was still wedged beneath his flesh. Sliding off the edge of the bed, he felt his feet try to slip out from under him, but forced them instead to do his bidding.

"Take me to her."

Clutching at the door, pulling himself upward, Wentworth threw himself toward the hall. Jackson thought for a moment to offer to help his employer move, but knew he should not. Any other person in the world would not only need such help, but insist upon it. Not Richard Wentworth, however. He wanted Jackson in front of him, leading him to his objective.

As they moved to the elevator at the end of the hallway, the chauffeur did not speak. He wanted to move more slowly, to encourage Wentworth to do so himself, to not further aggravate his wounds. He knew to so was not wise. Moving like a man possessed by some outside force, Wentworth threw one leg after another, woodenly, awkwardly, making his way down the hall through nothing more than grim determination. When there was but thirty feet remaining to the elevator, Jackson said;

"Just keep up that pace, major. I'm going to run ahead, press for the car. I'll hold it until you get there."

The chauffeur did as he said he would, mouthing a silent prayer of thanks when the thick elevator door slid forward before Wentworth arrived. As his employer half-walked, half-fell into the car, Jackson pressed for the correct floor, announcing that it was only two floors above.

Wentworth waited for the elevator door to close, watching it with the hostile intensity of a dog waiting for a dinner two days overdue. When the dark slab of steel finally slid out of the wall he was but seconds away from screaming. The ride up was no better. His head throbbing, eyes still not quite able to focus, Wentworth hung on through the strength of his will alone. Luckily for him the hospital elevator came equipped with a railing along all its walls for when the car reached the correct floor, the slight jolt it made when coming to a halt would have sent him to the floor if he had not been holding on with both hands.

"Which room? Take me there."

Again Jackson lead the way, offering no assistance. Those members of the hospital personnel the pair passed in the hall offered none as well. They had been overwhelmed that afternoon by the amount of the dead and the dying suddenly brought to their doors. Anyone moving under their own power, no matter how erratically, was doing better than the waves of brutalized victims they had seen that day.

Reaching the door to Nita's room, Jackson merely glanced in its direction, then pushed the door aside to allow Wentworth entry.

"You'd better brace yourself, major."

Staggering forward, Wentworth did as the chauffeur suggested. Indeed, he had been doing so since first the realization had struck him that she was not at his side. He had imagined her in every sort of ruinous state possible, forcing himself to consider the multitude of possibilities that might lie before her.

Never to walk again. Never again to dance in each others arms as they had so recently.

Her hearing destroyed. Never again to be able to play for her, to hear him tell her how much he loved her.

Blinded. Never to be able to see the sorrow in his eyes over the fact he had done this to her.

Approaching her bed, he shook as bitter grief washed through his mind, crippling his soul. Never had he seen her look so small. So fragile. Beneath her blanket, she somehow seemed almost waif-like. Shrunken.

Wentworth stared at her closed eyes, bruised and swollen. Her cracked, blood-stained lips. Broken nose, heavily bandaged face. All of her body that he could see, shoulders and neck, even her ears, were padded and bandaged. Her hair was in a wild disarray, what remained of it. Half of her glorious mane had been chopped away for some unknown reason leaving her looking like nothing more than an abused, abandoned doll.

A variety of tubes ran from hanging bottles, snaking underneath her blanket. Some led to her arms, some to her legs. Still others disappeared beneath her woolen shroud, their purpose only to be guessed.

Tears ran down Wentworth's cheeks as he stared at her. He did not sob, though. In fact, he made no noise at all. For how long he did so, he had no idea. Neither did Jackson. It was a moment frozen in time, a terrible instant which might have endured for days, or the blink of an eye.

Finally, however, Wentworth stirred, his movement so unexpected that Jackson actually stepped backward involuntarily. Not noticing, Wentworth bent forward gently, moving his face toward Nita's, pressing his lips to hers. He kissed her briefly, then pressed harder, his tears running down his cheeks, dribbling over both their mouths in quantity great enough to loosen the smears and crystals of Nita's blood clinging to her lips.

Drinking in the precious, scarlet drops, Wentworth swallowed, then stood erect once more and headed quietly for the door. Jackson followed, frightened by the terrible silence radiating from his employer.

The chauffeur had never considered himself a seer, but in that moment he could see the future clearly. And it contained more blood and death than any living being had ever known.

15

"SIR, what can I get you—" Wentworth waved his butler off, not bothering to speak, staggering past the older man, grateful to be once more within his own home. His head throbbing, his legs barely able to carry him, he cared not what any others wanted or needed from him at that moment. His sole concern was destroying those who had taken from him the only thing that mattered in his world.

As Jenkyns began to speak again, from behind their mutual employer, Jackson made several quick motions with his hand, indicating that trying to converse with Wentworth at that moment was not the best of ideas. As the two men entered Sutton Place, walking past the elderly butler, Jenkyns quietly shut the door behind them, then called out;

"Master Richard, turn around, if you would, sir." When Wentworth did not respond, his butler sucked down a deep breath, then spoke once more at the top of his voice;

"Master Richard, I believe I asked you to *turn around!*"

As both men stopped, the chauffeur freezing in his tracks, Wentworth blinking hard, fighting against the various voices swirling within his mind, Jenkyns moved forward, saying;

"You listen to me, good sir, I know exactly what is in your mind at this moment. Or more importantly, in your heart. Young Miss Nita is precious to me, as well. I have known love in my time. I understand what you are feeling. You could not be the man I know you to be if you were not thirsting now for revenge."

"I will—"

"You will *listen.*" By that point Jenkyns had moved himself directly in front of his long-time employer. His eyes filled with a fierce sympathy, he asked;

"Miss Nita still lives, does she not?" When Jackson confirmed that she was still hanging on, the older man nodded, his entire body shuddering at the news. His shoulders straightening as a great relief spread throughout his system, he said;

"Then, if there is hope for the one of you, I shall not lose the other. You, sir, are going to rest. Your wounds are not as great as hers, but they are sufficient to slow you down. If you go after those which have done this, you will die. If you rest and prepare, you will live. At least long enough to hold her in your arms once more."

Still did Wentworth remain silent, the warring voices within him continuing to struggle for supremacy. One part of him knew Jenkyns was correct. It sneered within his brain, reminding him that he could barely stand, that he was moving through sheer will power alone.

"You don't know who your enemy is," it reminded

him, "don't know where to find them. All you can do if you go out wounded and ill-prepared is make yourself a target, one not strong or quick enough to survive."

Sensible as the rational part of his mind was attempting to be, however, his passions would not be silenced. Laughing at his common sense, the driving part of his soul which he had kept in check for the previous three months was now raging forward, demanding that he throw himself into the fray once more.

"Do it," the voice of his alter-ego hissed. "What have you got left? What is there to lose? What matters your miserable life any longer? What will you do with it, how will you spend your remaining time ... without her?"

Bending over, shutting his eyes tight, Wentworth denied himself the easy pleasure of simply screaming in pain. His foes, he told himself, had not yet reduced him to an animal. Besides, he thought grimly, to scream would be to release the seething agony within his heart, to hurl it away from himself in a primitive attempt to make himself feel better. And that, he insisted, could not be allowed.

No. Instead, he would clutch hard his pain, embrace it, hone it to razor-sharpness, and then return it to those who had given it to him.

Straightening himself, shaking his head slightly, he moved to a chair there in his grand foyer and sat down. As he did so, he instructed Jenkyns to phone St. Christopher's and to check on Nita's condition. Standing off to the side, Jackson inquired as to whether or not there was anything he might do. Wentworth nodded, then said;

"Yes, fetch me a large Scotch. No matter what I learn in the next few minutes, I'll be needing one of those."

The chauffeur managed to complete his task far more quickly than the butler. Wentworth was not surprised. When he had walked out of the hospital the chaos in its hallways had been practically overwhelming. He was actually caught a bit off guard when Jenkyns returned as quickly as he did. A noncommittal look on his face, the old man said;

"She is still in very bad shape, sir. Still unconscious. But ... she lives."

Wentworth nodded, half his strength leaving his body as he did so. Having until that moment only sipped at the drink Jackson had brought him, he then tipped the tumbler back and drained its remaining contents, gulping from it the way a man stumbling forth from the desert might attack a glass of water.

Handing the glass to Jenkyns, Wentworth sat quietly for a long moment, then finally spoke.

"I am going to bed for a while. Admitting that I do not actually know how badly I am damaged, I can not say when I shall arise."

"Very good, sir. Most sensible. Simply tell us how we should occupy ourselves until you do."

"Where is Ram Singh?"

"Your most noble and violent friend is in the armory, sir, cleaning and loading weapons. Not knowing what you might require, but believing you would require something, he is making certain whatever you might want will be ready the moment you need it."

Wentworth nodded, a bit of relief curling around his despair. Turning to Jackson, he said;

"The Ford, the speed wagon ... get it ready. We're going to want to move fast."

"On it, major."

"And me, sir...?"

"Stock the larder for war." As Wentworth pushed himself up out of his chair, the butler asked;

"Nothing more, sir?"

"When I get up, I'll need a rare steak. Blood loss and all. But, being honest with myself for a moment, I know that won't be for a while. Besides, I should take a moment to thank you for, as so often in the past, once again providing me a sane harbor in an ocean of madness, for keeping me from crashing against the breakers of my own passions."

Clasping the older man on the shoulder, Wentworth said;

"Men *will* die for this. But, thanks to you, perhaps I'll be able to live long enough to make certain every single one of them dies. Right now, that's all I'm asking from life."

And then, Wentworth wearily staggered off in the direction of his bedroom. His every step a monumental struggle, he found himself moving slowly, simply so he would not fall down. As he continued forward, one careful step at a time, Wentworth shut down all the voices within his mind, dismissing his doubts.

Whether or not he did not act quickly enough, or at the right time, no longer mattered. What was done, was done. The past could not be changed.

"Only the future is ours to write," he reminded himself. Beginning the long climb up the stairs leading to his bedroom, Wentworth clutched the marble railing, proceeding slowly, each breath a gasp against the anguish of his movements. Smiling to himself through it all, though, he thought;

"Pain. Best thing about pain, it lets you know you're still alive."

And then, Richard Wentworth laughed aloud as he thought on just how many men he would soon be helping to feel as alive as possible.

16

THE PASSAGE of twenty-four hours found New York City in the grip of a terrible panic. Over the preceding three days, one after another monstrous hell from the past had been visited upon its citizens. Those attempting to find some semblance of comfort in the media were swiftly disappointed. To many it seemed as if their daily papers were competing with one another as well as both the local and national radio broadcasts in destroying all possible hope within the great city's citizens.

All of them dutifully listed their best estimates in dollars how much damage had been done, followed by their educated guesses at the number of dead, a figure by that point well into the thousands. Those whom in life had been held in high regard, or who possessed even the slightest amount of celebrity, were named repeatedly, the veiled hint that if such as they could die, what chance did the man in the street have of survival?

The next, for most outlets, was to then describe what had been done to the city the first time such terrors had been unleashed upon it, a statistical comparison of death rates old and new for any of their readers and listeners who might be keeping score. After that, with all possible facts hurled at the public repeatedly, their only recourse was to then shift forward into speculation.

What, they all wondered, would happen next? Here it was, they all announced, the fourth day of this still unexplained assault on New York City. What, they wondered with increasing ghoulish expectation, would the fourth attack be? What horror from the past would be unleashed next? When would it happen?

And, of course, where?

Headlines were increased to an overwhelming point size. Columns were filled on every front page leading to hundreds more in the following pages. Across the airwaves, endless amounts of time were given over to theorizing about what would come next? Would zombies again walk the streets of the city? Would the skies rain fire? Might the Green Globes of Death resurface, causing those it found to bleed all over until they died? Could the gas that stripped flesh from bones find its way into the city's avenues and back alleys once more?

As expected, before any gas could do so, panic filled the city's avenues and back alleys instead. Any who could leave New York did so in numbers so great traffic was snarled in every direction leaving the city. In only three days, even the most popular spots found their business dropping to practically nothing. Restaurants, movie houses, the theaters of Broadway—from the Statue of Liberty to Coney Island to the top of the Empire State Building—any place known for attracting groups now stood empty. Abandoned.

And, in such places, those who did gather spoke only in terms of despair. They had a right to do so.

Often when conversations centered on what could be done, someone or another who had somehow managed to cling to a few shreds of hope would remind their fellows that most likely, everything was going to be all right. Remember, they would say, each of the miseries being inflicted upon the city had been tried before. Every one of them, those which have been used in the new wave of assaults, and those the pundits are dragging up from the past, all of them have been stopped before. Every doomsday device unleashed, each of the terrorizing death machines thrown forward, they have *all* been conquered.

Such confidence would carry forth usually for only a handful of seconds before someone else engaged in the conversation, one of its less optimistic members, would point out that yes, indeed, the Green Fire and all the rest had been defeated when first they were used. By Police Commissioner Stanley Kirkpatrick, who now lingered at death's door in the hospital like so many others. And by the *Spider*—

Who was dead.

For years, since first the *Spider* had appeared, the police had condemned him. The newspapers had blazoned their front pages with calls for his capture. The radio commentators had bellowed over the shameful fact that such a monster was allowed to remain free. But, in the streets, the people had known better.

Those who had been pushed out of the way of bullets by him, who saw him endanger himself so they might live. The women who could look at their children, still healthy, still alive, because the *Spider* had risked his own life so theirs might be spared. The store owners who knew they would have lost all if the *Spider* had not arrived in time to stop those who would have taken everything they owned, perhaps murdering them at the same time.

Those who were being blackmailed, those who had been selected for slavery because of their beauty, or for death because they stood in the way of this or that rogue, those who had simply been in the wrong place at the wrong time, all of them, still alive, still breathing.

Because of the *Spider*.

Who now was dead.

This time, people knew that no savior was coming to protect them, that there would be no redemption. That this time, they were on their own.

As the fourth day dragged on, all could feel the building dread flooding the streets. In every house and apartment, in every tavern and bar, people waited for the next onslaught, waited to see what past terror would visit them, waited to see how many more would die.

Would die for nothing.

And that was what terrified the masses the most. That so far, it had all been for nothing.

Yes, those murdered on the train that first night had been robbed. But that, all agreed now, had been an opening salvo, one meant to mislead. After the planes and the bomb—after the death toll had rocketed upward to ten times what the first night had brought, and no demands had been put forth—what had started out as the normal amount of worry that came when some new madman attempted to put the city under its control, had now escalated to full blown terror.

Whoever was behind this latest string of atrocities did not seem to wish to profit from it. Twice now they had gone to great lengths, to obvious expense and trouble, to slaughter thousands. But, the people wondered, why? Most believed they would discover the answer to that question on the fourth day. Either that, or they would be subjected to another attack, one worse than the last.

And so, as the minutes piled one atop another, as the hours dragged by, from midnight to morning, from breakfast to lunch and onward into evening, their terror mounted. Everywhere, people nervously eyed their time pieces, watching the seconds tick off, one after another—

Waiting.

At Sutton Place, they waited also.

For over twenty hours, Richard Wentworth had slept uninterrupted. Apollo curled on the floor between his master's bed and the door, the master himself had remained in a deep slumber. At all times either Singh, Jackson or Jenkyns was in the room, sitting patiently, quietly. Watching.

Waiting.

At ten o'clock in the evening, Ram Singh came to replace Jenkyns. He would remain until two in the morning, when Jackson would take his place. Before the two switched places, they stood in the hallway for a moment, whispering so as not to disturb Wentworth. Holding the door open a crack so as to be able to hear any noise that might come from within, the butler asked;

"Nothing yet?"

"No," answered the Sikh in a whisper. "But two hours to go, and nowhere in the city has anything happened. The sheep on the radio can bray of nothing else. They are pathetic, but useful at least."

"What could they be waiting for?"

"Who can say," responded Singh, shrugging his thick shoulders. "Until the nature of their true goal can be discovered, how can anyone predict them? What will come to pass shall do so. And," Singh's face broke out in a wide grin as he finished, "when Sahib Richard awakens, retribution shall be made."

Jenkyns tilted his head slightly, nodding as he did so, then just before allowing the Sikh to go into Wentworth's bedroom, he said;

"These men ... 'they have sown the wind, and they shall reap the whirlwind.'"

And then the old butler turned and headed for his own room. His shift would come after Singh's and Jackson's. If things did not change, he would perhaps be able to manage six hours sleep. Then he would have to be up and about, taking care of his duties before it was his turn to once more sit and watch and wait.

Shutting the door, Singh padded quietly in his bare feet and took up his spot. Apollo raised his head long enough to make certain he approved on who had entered, then rested in upon his front paws once more.

And across the city, eyes stared at clocks, wondering what would happen next.

17

"NITA...?"

"Still unconscious, Major." Jackson rose from his chair, crossing to Wentworth's bed. "At least, that was the report last time we called. We've been checking every two hours. We stop at midnight. Start again at six."

Wentworth sat up, testing various muscles as he did so. Stretching his arms slowly over his head, straining them as far as he could, he asked;

"What time is it now? What day?"

"About three thirty in the A.M. You've been asleep a little over two days."

"I see." Wentworth lowered his arms as slowly as he had raised them, moving them in different directions to make certain he had his complete mobility. "What have our friends done in that time?"

"Our 'friends,' as you put it, haven't done anything." When Wentworth questioned Jackson's meaning, the chauffeur told him;

"Last two days, no more attacks. People are going out of their minds with worry. Panic is pushing folks over the edge, Major. They just don't know what to make of what's going on."

"Interesting."

Sliding off the edge of his bed, Wentworth continued to test his body with a series of slow movements, one by one straining each of his muscles, making certain he was restored enough to move against the city's latest menace. His confidence building as he discovered no more than a few minor aches, he mused aloud as he continued, saying;

"Quite possibly exactly what this new bunch is after. First, they introduce themselves to the city at large by bringing back the Green Fire. Then, after making people fear robbery, the next day they up the ante, making them simply fear for their lives."

"But on the third day, they merely do the same thing. Then they stop. What's their angle?"

"Perhaps they're more subtle than we think." Wentworth stopped speaking for a moment as he did a deep knee bend, only to discover that his left ankle was still somewhat tender. Rising out of the position slowly, he sat once more on the edge of his bed, resting for a moment as he said;

"Maybe their attacks are directed at the subconscious. First, make people afraid of transportation, of travel in vehicles. Second, make them afraid to even walk outside. Then, make them afraid of being indoors as well."

"You mean," said Jackson, snapping his fingers, "it's like they're saying, 'hey, nobody is safe from us no matter what they do.'"

"Precisely. Three days of terror. Then perhaps three days to think about it. To worry. Three days of waiting, of despair."

"This bunch," said the chauffeur, his brain racing, "they're really up to something new, aren't they?"

"That could very well be," agreed Wentworth. Standing once more, he continued, saying, "I've been putting all my concern forth toward Nita, which I'm certain you can understand, but tell me, is there any word on Stanley Kirkpatrick? Did he somehow manage to survive?"

"Amazingly, yes." Jackson spread his arms wide to signal his own surprise, telling Wentworth, "of course, there's no one who survived the explosion, that was inside the assembly hall, I mean, who can tell us what happened, you understand."

"Yes, go on—"

"The best the cops and all can figure, the people who were on the dais were protected somewhat because the flooring of the main auditorium's stage was constructed from solid steel." As Wentworth stood once more, the chauffeur told him;

"When the explosion went off, they think it lifted the entire stage, or at least most of it, and that caused the force to be spread outward in every direction. So, while everyone in the audience and outside were hit by shrapnel and all, those on the stage were mostly injured by the roof caving in."

"And Kirkpatrick's condition?"

"Better than Nita's, sorry to say. I mean, good for him, but, ahhhh ..."

"I know what you meant. Go on." Jackson lowered his head in embarrassment for a moment, then continued, saying;

"Word is Kirkpatrick, at least he's conscious some of the time. But, there's no way he's leaving the hospital anytime soon, though."

Wentworth nodded, then began a series of more vigorous movements, kicks and stretches which, while favoring his still tender left ankle, put a greater strain on his body, revealing to him all he needed to know about his current condition. As he did so, he ordered;

"I'll be leaving soon. Wake the others. Jenkyns needs to get to the kitchen. Steak, coffee. Fruit. Ram will accompany me. The Ford is ready?" When the chauffeur assured him it was, Wentworth nodded, adding;

"Good. Have Ram make certain the Ford is packed for a campaign of destruction. I'll meet the two of you in the dining room in twenty minutes."

Jackson said nothing, merely offering Wentworth a sharp salute before he exited. As he raced down the hall for Jenkyns' room, he wondered what Wentworth was planning. He himself had no idea what move they could make. In the two days he had waited with the others for Wentworth to awaken, he had thought long and hard as to what steps they could take. He had not been able to come up with anything that made any real sense.

But then, he reminded himself, he was not Richard Wentworth. Banging on Jenkyns' door, he added to that thought;

"Then again, *no one* is Richard Wentworth."

As he roused the household's butler, he offered up a short prayer of hope that, this time around, even Richard Wentworth could be enough.

WENTWORTH had eaten quickly, not only because he was ravenous, but because his time was short. Even moving as fast as he could, by the time he was ready to leave Sutton Place he had remaining not quite two hours of darkness with which to work before sunrise. With Ram Singh driving, he had departed his home riding in the back seat of the heavily armored Ford. He had dressed appropriately before leaving, of course, but had saved the task of assembling his alter identity for the ride, so as to save time.

A master of disguise, he worked in front of the mirror built into the back of the driver's seat although in truth he barely needed it for the mask he needed to create that morning. The putty he applied seemed almost to leap to his face. The greasepaint he worked in around it blurring the colors of skin and the added doughy cement so quickly as it might make an observer suspect magic might be involved.

Bit by bit the transformation occurred. The darkened, sunken eyes, the bulging, elongated nose, and the fitted celluloid points capping his canines, all of it came together in mere minutes. Still, though, there was more.

The wig fitted, and suddenly his head was covered by a wild and stringy shock of tangled, greasy hair. The small sack of cotton and sand strapped into place, and the line of his straight and perfect shoulders was ruined, made piteous and sinister with a stroke.

"We approach, Sahib."

"Good."

Wentworth allowed himself a fanged and sinister smile. His hands touching lightly the twin .45s strapped in place under each arm, the second pair buckled inside their holsters on the back of his belt, the rows of spare clips in their fitted leather slots. As Singh pulled the Ford up next to a fire hydrant, the only free spot on the block, Wentworth looked his image over one last time in the mirror, then slid its cover back into place, hiding it once more.

"I should not be long. Keep your eyes open. Be ready to move."

Nodding, one hand on the steering wheel before him, the other resting on the hilt of his great sword, stowed carefully between the driver's seat and door, the Sikh replied;

"I shall be all you need me to be, Sahib Richard. May evil learn the price for daring your wrath."

And then, the figure in the back seat silently slid out onto the sidewalk, a man none could mistake for Richard Wentworth. No, this was not him, perhaps not a man at all.

Standing next to the car, hunched, ugly and twisted, its skin sallow, its teeth fanged and discolored, this was something else. Garbed in a long black cape and floppy, wide-brimmed hat, this was not a man at all, but rather a repellent, vicious creature, a thing well-calculated to strike superstitious terror into the hearts of wrong-doers.

Looking up at the building it intended to invade, the ebony monstrosity paused long enough to release a flat and mocking laugh, then raced forward and disappeared into the shadows.

Sitting in the Ford, Singh smiled, a tiny grin at first that overwhelmed his face after a moment, forcing his lips apart so that he might unleash his own exultant gale of triumph. He worried not if any might hear him. It was still early in the morning. The streets were empty. With the windows of the Ford closed tight against the lingering cold of mid-March, he knew the sound would carry to no one. Besides, he cared not who heard him. His laughter was not self-amusement, but an announcement to the world. At long last—

The Spider was back!

"And woe," he said loudly, still chuckling as he did so, "to the wicked, for soon they are to die!"

18

"**W**AKE UP."

The man sprawled out across the top of the bed merely snored in response. His snores loud and deep, coupled with the facts that he was still dressed in his street clothing, had not bothered to crawl beneath his blanket despite the cold, and stank of alcohol, led the *Spider* to believe that his prey had been drunk when he had passed out. Picking up a cheap metal alarm clock from the small table next to the bed, the *Spider* caused the mechanism to go off, then dropped it on the man's face.

"Wha—"

The large man managed only the single syllable, fumbling at the clock, floundering as he tried to both shut the clanging alarm off and right himself. Not yet realizing he was not alone in his darkened room, he muttered;

"What the crap ... still dark? I didn't ... what—"

"Good morning, Mr. Johnson," came a sinister voice in response to his questions. "This is your wake up call."

Robert Johnson, a.k.a. Thump, froze in terror. The voice there in his quarters was not one he had ever heard before. Even if he had, however, it did not belong in his room. Fighting the waves of inebriation washing through his brain, the large man shook his head, desperately trying to reason out what was happening to him. The first thing he managed to recall was that he had been drinking with friends. In fact, he could remember no more than that. Try as he might, he could not even remember coming home. But, he was there. In the dark. His alarm clock ringing.

With someone else in his room—

"Who ... who's there?"

"Men call me the *Spider*."

Thump tried to find the revolver which he kept tucked within his belt, but he moved too slowly. Still hung over, half asleep, he searched his body, then sent his hands fumbling across the top of his bed, desperation slowly burning through the fog in his brain until suddenly a sharp pain connected with his skull.

"Looking for this?"

As Thump turned, howling as he did so, he saw a dark hand coming forward, holding his weapon out before him. Grasping for it clumsily, his brain still not functioning to the point where he might realize he was being played, he wrapped his large fingers around it, pulling it to himself. Taking an inordinately long time to get the revolver turned around and secured within a single hand, his finger on the trigger, he finally got it aimed at his intruder. His hand trembling, Thump swallowed hard, saying;

"You—you're dead."

"As you shall be, Mr. Johnson, if you do not answer my questions."

"What?"

"You are part of this gang which has descended upon New York. Murdering without reason. If you want to live, you will tell me everything you know. Otherwise, I shall enjoy the delightful pleasure of murdering you ... without reason."

His mind finally clearing to the point where he began to realize to exactly what level of danger his life had been elevated, Thump aimed his weapon as best he could and pulled the trigger. When nothing happened, he pulled it again, and again.

"There are no bullets in it, Mr. Johnson. I removed them."

The large man stopped pulling the trigger of his revolver. Still sitting on his bed, he stared at his weapon, turning it over in his hand as if his rum and beer-besotted brain could not understand what he had just been told.

"Now, Mr. Johnson, tell me the purpose of this new gang. Why do you do what you do? What is the plan?"

"Screw you!"

Thump launched himself off his bed in the direction of the *Spider*'s voice. He managed to almost touch the black blur which stepped out of his way, allowing him to crash into the wall. Despite the fact he had hit hard enough to shatter the plaster and severely dent the metal mesh holding it to the wall, the large man turned instantly, swinging his empty revolver in wide arcs. Calmly waiting for his arm to pass, the *Spider* stepped in close to Thump, striking him on the chin with the flat of his palm.

The large man staggered backward, his spine slamming against the same wall he had just dented. Not allowing him a moment's relief, the *Spider* moved forward, striking him again—in the ear, the eye, the neck. All painful, but not crippling, blows. The gun fell from Thump's hand, bouncing loudly across the uncarpeted floor. The large man slid to the floor, screaming in pain. His screeches stopped as the *Spider* grabbed him by the hair and slammed his head against the wall.

"Quiet now, Mr. Johnson. People are trying to sleep."

When Thump merely began to growl, his arms sloppily grabbing for his assailant, the *Spider* rammed his head forward once more, then once again, shoving it far enough into the metal mesh to both tangle his hair and cut into his skin.

"Owwwww, owwwwwwww, my Christ," screamed Thump, pushing awkwardly against the wall, trying to extract himself without causing himself any further pain, "Get me outta here!"

"No problem at all, Mr. Johnson."

Catching hold of the skin at the back of Thump's neck, the *Spider* pulled harshly, ripping the larger man's head free. Thump left quite a number of strands of hair behind, blood flying through the air as he was hurled across the room. The *Spider* aimed him at his dresser, making certain the center of his back came against its nearest corner. Thump's eyes came open wide as he made contact, his tongue jamming forth, spittle frothing up and over his lips. Falling in a tangled heap onto the floor, the big man pulled himself to his elbows, pleading;

"Please, no more. What'dya want from me. I don't know nuthin'."

The *Spider* stood above his victim for a long moment, holding himself in check. On the floor before him kneeled a creature that epitomized everything he had come to loath in humanity. Stupid, slovenly, grasping, willing to terrorize others, deprive them and their families of everything they had worked years for if it meant nothing more than a moment's pleasure for him. He wished he did not, but he knew how Thump's mind worked. Knew that when he robbed, the big man did not think of it as stealing, but that he was merely getting his own due back.

"You're wondering why I'm doing this to you, aren't you, Mr. Johnson?" The *Spider* bent closer, whispering his words to the figure cowering on the floor.

"After all, you've never done anything really wrong, have you? Most likely, whatever you've done, whatever you've stolen, you've felt entitled to do so."

The *Spider* caught hold of Thump's chin, and then wrenched his head painfully around until their eyes met, one set blazing with a cold and calculating anger, the other red and filled with tears. Dragging the big man's face even closer, the *Spider* demanded in a hissing voice;

"Answer me!"

"Yes, yes," blurted Thump. "It's true. It—"

The big man tried to say more, then suddenly gulped, his eyes bulging. Knowing what was coming, the *Spider* pushed his victim aside, allowing him to vomit forth the churning excesses of the previous evening. Slipping as he fell, Thump spewed both the remains of his dinner and the drinking binge which had followed across his apartment floor, falling face forward into his own torrent.

Unable to provide any further resistance, the large man remained where he had fallen, not trying to extricate himself from the stinking pool. He was, simply, too tired to move. Too frightened to move. Stepping close to the big man once more, the *Spider* told him;

"I'm glad you're willing to admit you understand this idea of entitlement. Because, you see, Mr. Johnson, I'm feeling a bit entitled myself right now."

Thump made one last attempt to rise, struggling with all his remaining strength to push himself up out of his filth and begin crawling for the door, but the *Spider* pulled one of his .45s and cracked the big man across the head with it. Thump went down once more, but stayed down this time.

"I'm feeling entitled to everything you know about your new employers. The name of their organization. What they plan to do next. How they obtained the weapons of the past. What others they might have. I'm feeling entitled to all sorts of information, Mr. Johnson. And you're going to give it to me."

"But, but," Thump sputtered weakly, flecks of drying sputum flying from his lips, his voice weak and pitiful, "I mean, I don't ... they don't ... I don't know all that kinda stuff."

"We'll see," answered the *Spider*. Flashing Thump a wide grin, one that conveyed the message that its owner was almost hoping to be disappointed, he added;

"We'll see."

And then, the torture began.

19

"WHERE NEXT, SAHIB?"

Shutting the back door to the Ford behind himself, Wentworth stole a quick look at the sky. With the sunlight already beginning to steal over the lower East Side's rooftops, he thought for a moment, then answered with a touch of resignation;

"Home. For now."

Ram Singh did not question his instructions. He knew Wentworth must have gathered at least some of the information he had wanted—he had been gone too long to have done otherwise. He also knew his employer would most likely need time to digest whatever he had learned so as to be able to plan their next moves. Also, superior being that Richard Wentworth was, still did the Sikh appreciate that during the previous few days the man had been through a great deal. That he was carrying an enormous amount of weigh on his shoulders.

Besides, Singh had seen the large man's body fall from above to splatter sloppily against the sidewalk. It was but the barest of beginnings, only a slight evening of the overwhelming balance due between good and evil. But, it was enough to make the Sikh grin in anticipation of what awaited the rest of the thug's compatriots in the near future.

As for Wentworth, he had indeed learned much of what he wanted to know. And, all of it he found worrisome. Unlike so many of the gangs he had faced in the past, this one appeared to well organized and efficient. The gang had no official name. It did have a leader, but Thump had never met the man in person, nor did he have any name for the individual outside of "the Boss."

What Wentworth had found interesting was the fact the Boss had structured his gang much along the order of a typical resistance underground. None of the gang members knew more than a few of the others. Thump, for instance, had been part of the squad that had murdered and robbed those on the train. He knew many of the others involved in that night's activities personally, and had rushed to give the *Spider* their names, addresses, and anything else he knew about them. But, those who had flown the planes, or who had planted the explosives at the assembly hall, details like this were completely unknown to him.

"You gotta believe me," the large man had whined pitifully, eyes tearing, nose leaking, his voice cracking like that of a frightened teenager. "None of us knows nuthin' more than we got told. Like, I mean, like when they gassed the city, or blowed up that building, they didn't even tell us to stay away from the places where that stuff was gonna happen. 'Stay home,' they told us, and gave us the times and all, but they didn't say nuthin' more."

The *Spider* believed him. The large man was simply too frightened to be lying. He confirmed, without being asked, his captor's earlier suspicion that the original three days of violence were then being followed with three days of calm. Thump also told him that on the seventh day, another three days of attacks would begin.

"And no, I don't know what's gonna happen then—I don't. I swear!"

The *Spider* had merely squatted over the big man, staring intently. Turning his head, spit drooling from his mouth, his voice was a whimper as he added;

"All I know is, me, and the other guys what I told you about before, it'll be our turn up at bat again. Tomorrow, I mean. We're just supposed to go to this warehouse on the west side, down in the meat packing district. Eight o'clock in the morning. Just like the first time, we'll get our instructions, and then go do what we're told."

"You expect me to believe," the *Spider* had snarled at that point, "that you were handed the apparatus needed to make the Green Fire functional, and then merely told to go forth and use it without training?"

"No, no!" Thump had scrambled away from his interrogator at that point, fearing what the tone in his voice implied. Scuttling across the floor like a damaged crab, he blindly ran into the wall, screeching when he did so. Then, pressed up against the cracked surface, more tears came to his eyes as he added;

"No, we were just the muscle. Brian, he told me, the Boss has like this science team, see. Those guys, they set things up all the time. But then when everything's set, they get those guys outta the picture and send us in to do the rough stuff."

By that point the *Spider* had known he had wrung all the information out of Thump that the man possessed. The Boss, whoever he might be, was indeed a clever foe. His plans were not known to the rank and file. His top men were unknown to them as well. Only the lieutenants he hired, men like Brian Carnahan who had organized thugs like Thump and his fellows, were known—and then, only to their own men. The large man had not even been certain if Carnahan knew any of the other group leaders. He was certain Carnahan had no idea to the identity of the Boss.

He did, however, know what had happened to the man with the crescent-shaped scar after his and Thump's run in with Tito Caliepi.

"That fiddler, the bastard ... he tore Brian's damn eye right outta his face."

From the way Thump shuddered, the *Spider* had been certain the thug remembered all too well the feel of the eyeball as it had bounced against his own face. As the *Spider* merely stared impassively, the big man had continued, saying;

"But, at least it was clean. A lotta the gang got taken out that night. Pissed the Boss off, too, we heard. But, this next attack, it's gonna be different from the first."

"How so?"

"That night we did the train, it was like only one train—right? This time, there's gonna be three teams. Now, like I said, I ain't got no idea what we're gonna do, but the Boss promoted one of us guys that survived the other night, and he got together with the other guys in charge, and—"

"Get to the point, Mr. Johnson."

Quickly, Thump explained as best he could that all of the lieutenants had met and traded men around until they had three squads ready for whatever was to take place next. By pulling in some reserves the Boss had kept in case of an emergency, in the end his trio of ten man units had been reduced only slightly, to nine men apiece, a number he apparently found sufficient for his purposes. Thus, on the one hand, because of Caliepi's tangling with the thugs he had discovered, Thump had been given access to information he would not have had otherwise.

On the other hand, he whined, it meant he no longer knew who his own lieutenant was. Carnahan had been taken away to be given care. At least, that was what Thump and the others had been told. The big man was not certain what he had been told was the truth, but he was certain what might happen if he were to question the Boss. Even if it meant that the next time the large man worked for this new gang, even if it meant doing so without *any* of the men from his usual gang, he would do so without hesitation.

Carnahan had been removed from the picture, and his gang had been split up and reformed. That was apparently good enough for Thump, who valued his neck far more than he did whatever level of friendship he had held for the man with the crescent-shaped scar.

As he had told the last part of his story, however, the *Spider* had noticed something different about Thump's attitude. Slowly, bit by bit, the man had been summoning his nerve. He had made certain to continue to beg and moan and plead in fear, but the *Spider* knew the kind of man with whom he was dealing. Had seen far too many cornered rats to not know what was swimming within the big man's mind.

At first—half-drunk, disoriented, in pain—Thump had spilled his guts as quickly as he could, revealing everything he knew in a desperate bid to get his wits pulled together. As time wore on, and the large man began to realize he was running out of information, however, he had begun to try and formulate an escape. Realizing what the man was up to, though, the *Spider* had allowed him to believe he was being clever.

As he told the last part of his story, Thump had edged as slowly as possible closer and closer to his bed. Having checked the thug's room before he had awakened the big man, just as he had emptied Thump's gun, the *Spider* had also made note of whatever other defenses the thug had at hand.

A more charitable individual might have warned the killer that his efforts were futile, but there was no charity to be found within the breast of the man in black standing over Thump that morning. Waiting for what he believed would appear to the large man to be his best moment to attack, the *Spider* had allowed a softer note to enter his voice, as if he were feeling more kindly toward his victim. Then, he had turned his back, and waited for the inevitable.

At once the big man had reached under his bed to pull free the knife he kept nestled within its open springs. Pulling the large blade free, he had scrambled to his feet and lunged, only to find the *Spider* waiting for the move. With a casual disdain, the avenger had caught hold of the thug's arm and twisted, sending the knife dropping to the floor. Then, he had twisted the arm in the other direction and added a push, sending Thump flying head-first for the room's only window.

Descending to the ground quickly, the *Spider* had signaled Ram Singh to drive forward. The Sikh did so with ease, then left the motor running as he jumped out of the Ford to help stow what remained of Thump within its trunk. After that, he had slid back behind the wheel of the powerful roadster and asked;

"Where next, Sahib?"

Shutting the back door to the Ford behind himself, Wentworth had stolen a quick look at the sky. With the sunlight stealing over the rooftops already, he answered;

"Home. For now."

He had not learned nearly as much as he had hoped

he might. But, he thought, he had learned enough. The city had one more day to breathe easy, which meant he had one full day to prepare.

His mind racing as the Ford rolled through the relatively quiet early morning streets, he planned to make the most he could of every minute of that one full day.

20

AFTER arriving home, Wentworth had retired to his study while Ram Singh disposed of Thump's shattered remains. Unlike the past, this time there would be no leaving of his body for the police to discover, ominously marked by the vermillion seal of the *Spider*. For the moment the criminologist was determined that no one realize his alter ego walked the streets once more. It was the single ace he was holding, and considering the game being played in his city at that moment, he meant to drive the table stakes up a great deal higher before allowing his only trump card to be revealed.

"Three ..."

Checking the warehouse address he had been given by the late Thump, he had studied the lists of businesses and the such which made up the area in detail, trying to determine what the Boss's plans for the next day might be. Nothing practical presented itself to him, however. There were too many variables to consider, especially once he factored in the idea that there were to be three squads of men attacking the city at once.

"Three ..."

Wentworth rolled the number over in his head, studying the various maps of the city spread out across his desk. He had studied the various boroughs of New York together and individually. He had also looked at the problem from the standpoint of the city's subway systems, its waterways, roadways and its airports, but no one idea presented itself to him as being better than any other.

Finally surrendering, giving up any hope of predicting the Boss correctly in the face of the overwhelming amount of possibilities, Wentworth turned his attention to other matters. First, he made certain Sutton Place was well defended, setting Jenkyns to making certain every window was screened and locked, every outer doorway barred, and that all of their other standard anti-siege measures were securely in place.

Second, he set Jackson to rounding up a team of trustworthy men that would be able to help defend their home if need be. Taking into consideration that at least one of the Boss's lieutenants had been aware of Tito Caliepi, had considered him a connection to the *Spider*, it worried the criminologist that this new gang may be planning an invasion of his home.

During his decades as the *Spider*, Wentworth had, on more than one occasion, been accused of being such, both by the police and the elements both he and the police opposed. His home had been plundered, even destroyed, more than once. Sooner or later, he knew, he would be forced to reveal the renewed existence of the *Spider* to this latest menace. They were far too well organized, far too powerful for him to stop without eventually stepping into the spotlight. It was, the criminologist realized, an inevitability.

Toward that end, he wanted to be ready. He would not see his home destroyed again. Yes, on the one hand it was merely a collection of possessions—material things which could be replaced, which did not matter if they could not. But, within Sutton Place were people as well. People he would not see harmed.

And, on a deeply personal level, he would not see it damaged in any way at all because it was there that he had last seen Nita. It was the place that he meant to be the home they would share for the rest of their lives. Thus he was determined that it would be, if at all possible, on the day when she was finally capable of returning to it, in every way, exactly as she remembered it. Down to the last stick of furniture.

And so, to that end, Jackson was instructed to gather those he could find to become a household security force. The majority of them would patrol the grounds. Those few privy to certain of Sutton Place's secrets would assist the chauffeur in defending the interior.

After that, Wentworth left his home in Jenkyns and Jackson's hands, departing for St. Christopher's with Ram Singh driving. Going directly to the floor where Nita still rested, unconscious, hovering ever so tenuously between life and death, he entered her room while Singh remained in the hall outside, standing guard against any who might intrude upon their time together.

Knowing his duty, the great Sikh would make certain that none entered her room for as long as his employer remained inside. Even doctors and nurses would be turned away until his friend had finished.

Standing over her bed, Wentworth stared down at the broken, suffering form of the woman he loved, his emotions threatening to overwhelm him. Even his keen ears could barely pick up the sound of her breathing, so slight a sound had it become. The color of her bruises, those in spots which were visible to him, did seem to have lessened in intensity, but that was the only favorable sign he could detect.

Everything else about her remained the same. A quick study of her chart revealed all to Wentworth's trained intellect. She had not regained consciousness since she was first admitted. Her pulse, weak when she arrived, had grown steadily weaker. She had received regular check-ups, examinations to test whether or not her condition had improved enough for them to be able chancing operating on her. So far, she had not shown even the slightest improvement. Which meant, not only was Nita Van Sloan in danger of dying if she did not receive the operation she needed to repair her damaged organs, but also that such an operation itself could kill her.

Wentworth stood beside her bed for an agonizing long amount of time, then finally bent low so that he might speak so that only she might hear. He understood, of course, that it was most likely she would hear nothing at all, but that was of no concern. He simply had things which he wished to say to her, things he could not leave without at least *trying* to let her know.

Afterward, he returned to the hall, rejoining Singh. As the Sikh stood quietly, awaiting orders, the criminologist took a moment to regain his composure. Finally, sucking down a deep breath, he told his friend;

"As you know, I sent Jackson to find a small army to defend Sutton Place."

"It is our home," responded Singh. "It is filled with valuable things. More to the point, it should not be that our very domicile is allowed to be fouled by infidels."

"True," agreed Wentworth. "The things we value should be protected." The criminologist waited for the Sikh to nod, then added;

"Which is why I am leaving you here, to guard Nita."

Ram Singh said nothing. A lesser man might have protested. Indeed, considering that those of his sect did not even consider women as beings which possessed souls, it would not have been unreasonable for the great warrior to have been insulted by such a command. But, Singh knew better.

Wentworth, he knew, was about to throw himself into a fray possibly worse than any he had ever faced. At that moment, none of them knew what they were up against. The only thing they actually knew for certain was that somehow their enemy had gained control of a number of the most terrible weapons anyone had ever faced. How many of these death machines from the past they possessed within their arsenal was a matter strictly for conjecture. The Sikh was well aware of the hideous fact that for all they knew, the Boss and his gang might have access to every doomsday device over which the *Spider* had ever triumphed.

To strive against such odds, and somehow prevail, Singh knew, Richard Wentworth was going to have to disappear. Only the *Spider* could prevail against the forces waiting for him, and if there was doubt within the mind he shared with the criminologist, then it was possible he might not be able to triumph. Nodding, allowing himself the slightest of self-satisfied smirks, the Sikh held out his key ring to Wentworth, telling him;

"You remember, I am certain, Sahib, where the car is parked. I shall remain here as you have ordered, and I make you this promise. If those forces of Destiny which control us all decide that the end of days has come for Miss Nita, there is nothing I can do, for I am but a man, and as much a toy in the hands of the gods as any other. However, if anything lesser than a god comes for her, no matter how large or powerful, or in what numbers, if it possesses flesh, if it can be made to bleed, then these halls shall run red. Scarlet rivers will flood the stairwells, A mountain of bodies shall be piled. Their death cries will fill the valleys of Hell."

Singh pulled open the left-hand side of his overcoat ever so slightly, just enough to reveal the sight of his great sword. Giving Wentworth the same short but proud smile he had a moment before, he let his coat close, saying quietly;

"Clear your mind of concern. She is safe. No harm will come to her. Now, go—do what must be done. I shall do the same. And when this is done, and all I have said has come to pass, we will breakfast at DiVicos to rejoice our good fortune."

Wentworth nodded, once—sharply—then turned and headed back to the elevators. With Nita as safe as anyone could possibly be, he had but one last task to which he needed to attend. And then, after that, he would be at war.

A war which, although he had no way of knowing then, would determine the fate of the entire world.

21

"RICHARD," exclaimed Kirkpatrick, his voice weak, but enthusiastic, "come in, come in."

Wentworth had left Nita's room and headed for the commissioner's, wanting to check on his friend for a number of reasons. First and foremost, Stanley Kirkpatrick *was* his friend. Despite the number of times the commissioner had attempted to prove the criminologist was indeed the fearsome public enemy known as the *Spider*, they had known each other for decades, and their respect for one another was immense.

He also wanted to know in exactly what kind of shape Kirkpatrick was at that moment. Was he strong enough to still maintain control over the vast army which was the police department of New York City? Wentworth hoped he was, for the criminologist had a bold plan he hoped to put into effect, and having Kirkpatrick in his corner, and not some low level political appointee thrust into his position instead, was key toward making it work.

"I intend to, old friend," answered Wentworth. "Although I won't be staying long. But I would like to chat for a moment, if you're up to it? Just a couple of personal matters, if you don't mind ..."

Understanding that Wentworth was requesting privacy, the commissioner chuckled as if he expected his friend to tell him some kind of off-color story, then dismissed the two officers stationed within his room for protection. After the door had shut firmly behind the pair, he said;

"That what you had in mind?"

"You know me too well."

Kirkpatrick motioned for his visitor to pull a chair over closer to his bedside. Then, satisfied that they would be able to speak without being overheard, he lowered his voice to ask;

"Nita ... has there been any ... improvement?"

Kirkpatrick let the question hang, knowing that to embellish it further might simply cause his friend unneeded grief. Nodding, Wentworth told the commissioner all he knew of his fiancée's condition, then asked his friend what he might be able to tell him of the explosion in the assembly hall. Although Kirkpatrick was willing to share all he knew from his first hand experience at ground zero of the blast, as well as all that had been reported to him since then, he was able to supply Wentworth with nothing much in the way of new information.

After that, the criminologist inquired as to how Kirkpatrick's own health was at the moment. The commissioner confirmed that he was able to run much of his office's business from his hospital room. Although he disagreed with their diagnosis, Kirkpatrick's doctors insisted he was too weak to leave St. Christopher's. However, so far his precinct captains and their lieutenants had been able to cover for him, so the idea of replacing him, even temporarily, had not yet been suggested by city hall. Thus his hospital room had become more of a war chamber than anything else, with runners constantly bringing him information, and then being dispatched back to the front lines.

"Not that there's been much new information coming in the last few days ..."

"That's about to change."

Kirkpatrick studied Wentworth's face for a moment, staring at him long and hard. Their eyes locking, the commissioner took a moment to build his strength. Then, a thin smile spreading across his face, he asked;

"How?"

Leaning closer, lowering his own voice, Wentworth told the story of what he had been doing since the explosion. Editing his version of the truth, he told Kirkpatrick that he had managed to track Thump down through the details gathered from the witnesses questioned at Krenkel's. After that, he admitted to his confrontation with the thug, leaving out any mention of the *Spider*, but telling him everything he had learned.

"All right, then," said the commissioner, a hopeful fire

blazing to life within his eyes, "this is certainly something more than we had. Still ... I don't suppose you've tumbled to any kind of a notion as to what they're up to? What they want?"

"No—not the slightest, Stanley," admitted Wentworth. "And, I assume you know how sorry I am to have to admit that."

"Of course. Now, tell me what you've come up with to do about it."

"Well, you're certainly showing a great deal of faith in me."

Kirkpatrick made to answer, then suddenly fell into a great coughing fit. Struggling to control himself, he gripped at the railing on his bed, his body shaking as he clenched his teeth together, fighting to stop the attack. When he finally had himself under control, the commissioner signaled that he needed a moment to compose himself.

Watching his friend quietly, Wentworth observed that the short burst had severely weakened Kirkpatrick. Sweat had broken out across his forehead. His eyes had lost much of their light, his cheeks suddenly far more ashen. Sinking into his pillows, his voice infused with a far raspier tone, he waved the criminologist to move closer to his bed, then told him;

"Listen to me ... when the coughing starts, it only gets worse. I'll be doing it again soon, it'll keep up, then I'll be out once more. Before that happens, tell me what it is you have in mind."

As quickly as possible, Wentworth outlined his plan. As he listened, Kirkpatrick did the best he could to not allow his injuries to get the best of him. Straining to stave off another coughing fit, to remain conscious, he managed to hear out the criminologist's idea before he succumb once more. When his second fit had passed, he called for one of the guards to return.

The commissioner then, working through Wentworth, outlined a tactical strategy for the next morning. The criminologist gave the sergeant a small box he had brought with him, and then Kirkpatrick dismissed the officer so he might carry out his instructions.

After that, knowing his friend was weak, Wentworth suggested that he be leaving. After all, they would both need all their strength come the next day if his plan were to succeed. Kirkpatrick agreed, but said;

"Happy to get rid of you so I can get some of that rest everyone says I need, but ... I want to talk to you first."

"Whatever, Stanley," answered Wentworth. "What is it?"

"This thing you're planning, it is a bold ... and obviously ... very dangerous thing."

"Yes, but—"

"Richard, listen to me." Kirkpatrick gasped for air, wheezing from the effort of simply cutting his friend off. A bit of color returning to his cheeks, he took one last deep breath, then started again, saying;

"What you are thinking of doing ... it could very well work. But, I don't believe you are strong enough, skilled enough, to pull it off."

"With all due respect, if not me, then who? Who else would you trust? Who else would you send?"

Kirkpatrick swallowed hard. Looking at the door, his eyes scanned its edge, making certain it was flush, that there was not the slightest possibility anyone might be listening to them. Then, in the most hushed whisper he could produce, he said;

"You are a brave and resourceful fellow, and we both know it's true that I owe my life to you several times over.

But ... Richard Wentworth is not the man for this job. For something like this ... you need to send in ... the *Spider*."

Wentworth stared at the commissioner as if he had lost his mind. Undeterred, Kirkpatrick added;

"I'm not looking for a confession. I don't want you to say anything. Just listen to me. Yes, we've danced around each other for years. I have, in my time, allowed my sense of duty to a static idea of the law overwhelm my common sense. But, I only ask you to remember the various times when I actually had the *Spider* within my grasp. When I turned my back for no sensible reason and allowed him to escape—"

"Stanley, I ..."

"When I had my gun drawn, aimed at his heart ... and yet did not fire."

"You don't ..."

"Richard ... I applaud you for trying to walk away from it all. I've thought long and with much consideration these past months ... I have weighed the actions of the *Spider* and found him wanting in no way. Although his measures are harsh, too harsh for the gentle sensibilities of those who dictate how society shall run, he has far too often been what was needed, and—"

Again Kirkpatrick broke into a long and violent series of hacking coughs, a misery so intense that each grating bark actually caused his body to shake within his bed. Tears broke free from his eyes, the massive force of the attack leaving him weaker than ever. Pulling himself together, sensing he would slip away from the conscious world in only a few moments, he cleared his throat as best he could, then said;

"And ... we need him now."

Wentworth had no idea what he might say in response.

He trusted Kirkpatrick as he might a brother. But still, to simply admit he was the *Spider*, the idea seemed practically incomprehensible to him. Searching for any words with which he might respond, the criminologist blinked hard, made a small motion with his hands as if he were about to speak, then went silent as Kirkpatrick added, his voice just slightly more forceful;

"For the good of the city, he must be brought forward. These men, these new fiends, they're not just crooks. Nor simple blackmailers. They're up to something new— something unlike any thing we have ever faced before."

Breaking off speaking, moving a hand to cover his mouth, the commissioner tightened his whole body suddenly, willing himself not to cough again, choking down the natural inclination. His face contorted grimly against his pain, Kirkpatrick forced himself to speak, saying;

"These bastards ... they're monsters. They're insane. And they, they must be stopped. Because, I truly believe ... these men are not just a danger to New York ... but to everyone. To all men ... to the *world*."

Small bubbles of foam flecked along the line of the commissioner's lips, forming in response to his internal struggle. Finally, his most recent fit having passed for a moment, still Kirkpatrick could sense his body rapidly losing what little strength he had remaining. Desperate, feeling his few sparks of energy deserting him, he added;

"You must do it, Richard. For your sake, for Nita—for the good of all—you must unleash ... the *Spider*!"

And then, the commissioner slipped back into unconsciousness. Which meant, if Kirkpatrick was correct, Richard Wentworth had been left to decide the fate of humanity on his own.

22

THE LARGE MAN walked along the front of the warehouse, studying the outside of the building, searching for its entrance. The series of plain metal structures running along the wharf front were exceedingly similar, with only their stencil-painted numbers allowing one to differentiate one from the other. The big man was not worried about finding the warehouse he wanted, however. Judging by the string of men all heading for the same doorway, he assumed he knew where he needed to go. His assumption soon proved correct.

"Hey, Thump ... over here."

The large man threw a wave at the fellow who had called out to him. Walking toward him slowly, he said in a lowered, scratchy voice;

"Hey, didn't see ya."

"You don't sound so good. You gonna be able to play a whole game?" Nodding weakly, the large man said;

"Yeah, musta just ate a bad oyster last night. Stomach's all screwy. I'll be jake."

Both men entered the warehouse, heading through a corridor created by numerous large packing crates at the direction of a harsh-looking individual who stopped everyone at the door. Some were forced to show some manner of identification. The guard seemed to know the large man and his friend, and merely waved them through. As they made their way to the center of the warehouse, the smaller of the pair asked;

"So, what'dya think it's gonna be this time?" When the big man said nothing, his friend replied, "Awwwww, com'on, you can tell yer old pal Hickey."

"I don't know ... somethin' that kills people?" The shorter man let loose a loud guffaw. Looking at his companion with admiration, he said;

"Damn, you can't be too sick if you can crack that wise. Good one, Thump."

The larger man smiled weakly, then allowed the short fellow to chatter along, a task for which he seemed well suited. He was only able to speak for a handful of seconds more, however, before the pair reached a clear area in the center of the warehouse. As they and the several others behind them came into the light, a man dressed in a dark suit holding a clip board called out;

"Good. It appears everyone is here. I commend you all for being punctual. You may refer to me as Mr. Henson. Now, getting straight to business, as you know, the Boss rewards those who follow orders. And we have some very interesting orders for you this morning."

The nine who made up that morning's team were signalled to move closer to the table in the center of the open area. Something rested on the table covered over with a dark tarp. As the men moved in around it as directed, the largest of them looked at his watch then scowled. The big man poked at it twice, then shook it. As he checked it once more, he seemed pleased with the results of his poking, and lowered his arm once more. As he did, his friend commented;

"Fancy watch, Thump."

Before either man could say anything else, however, Henson called for everyone's attention. Then, as two other men, both wearing white smocks and rubber gloves, began to remove the tarp, the one in charge announced;

"This is the ticket, today, gentlemen. Gather around and take a look, because this morning you're all going to get to play Buck Rogers."

"Huh, and me a Flash Gordon fan."

The jokester's comment was ignored by all. The man in the dark suit had a schedule which he needed to keep. He would not have any trouble doing so, however. That which lay exposed on the table before the nine summoned forward, including the comedian, had stunned them all into silence. Tapping his clipboard against that which had just been uncovered, Henson said,

"Like everything else the Boss has thrown at the city so far, this item too comes from the past. But this morning, in less than an hour, it shall cease being history as you gentlemen bring it forward into the present."

The nine stared, some of them recognizing what it was they were seeing, most of them not. The large man, however, knew exactly, in quite precise detail, what it was stretched out on the table before them all.

It appeared to be nothing more than a somewhat stylized, modern suit of armor. Remarkably shiny, smoothly jointed, its helmet a bubble large enough to encompass any head, the suit seemed as if it might have been taken directly off the cover of a hundred different science fiction pulp magazines. Taking note of an extremely sinister rifle on the table next to the armor, the big man asked;

"This looks like the get-up they called the Accursed Light. Goes back five, six years, don't it?"

"Correct, Thump. Very good."

"Spits fire, right?"

"Not exactly," answered Henson. "The beam your weapon emits will burn a man alive far better than mere fire. In fact, improved as they are, these weapons will now burn through much more than simple flesh and bone." The man in the suit stared at the big man for a moment, then added;

"You appear to have a somewhat more agile mind than I might have given you credit for, Thump. What else can you tell us about this weapon?"

"Well, Mr. Henson, the only other thing I really remember from back then is that these rifles, the beams they shoot, I mean, wasn't it like they could be stopped by dry ice crystals? If that's the case, won't the cops be able to put the kibosh on us pretty quick?"

"Excellent question," answered Henson. Tapping the armor with his clipboard once more, he said;

"But the Boss is ready for anything. The Accursed Light projectors' vulnerability to something as simple as dry ice made them a ridiculous weapon. But, the Boss's scientists have fixed that problem." Pointing toward one of the men in the white smocks, Henson said;

"Why don't you explain it to them, Bergen?"

Quickly the shorter of the two technicians delivered a brief monologue detailing the changes made to the weapon since it had last been used. The rifle's beams could no longer be stopped by dry ice. The metal suits had been made, not only lighter, but bullet-proof as well. The helmets were mirrored, so that those wearing the armor could see out clearly in all directions, but their faces were completely hidden from view.

The nine nodded absently as the technician spoke, most of them simply staring at the armor before them as well as its menacing assault weapon. At a call from Henson, other white-garbed men began wheeling forward more sets of armor. As each of the nine was presented with their own suit, Henson explained;

"You will, each of you, be bolted into your suit. Then, your instructions today are simple. At nine o'clock, you will simply walk out the door through which you came in, and kill as many people as you can for fifteen minutes. You are to stay as close together as you can, for when the fifteen minutes has passed, a truck will come in to pick you up. It will be large, yellow, and it will be flashing its headlights. You will have three minutes to get aboard or be left behind."

"That's not very long," said the large man, "ah ... only fifteen minutes to kill guys, I mean."

"No, it's not," agreed Henson. "But it will serve. The city is on edge. They're all out there, shaking. Waiting for something to happen. The dread that has been building will push people over the edge. And besides, don't forget, there are three teams. People will be slaughtered in multiple spots."

As each of the nine was helped into their suits, the layers of rubberized metal hung in place and adjusted to each individual's body, the large man asked;

"So, when you say kill as many people as we can, should we go anywhere in particular? I mean, who should we be killin'?"

"Law enforcement of any kind, children, as always, they're always good for headlines," mused Henson. "But this warehouse was picked for a reason. We are directly across from the very heart of the docks. Thus, your main targets today are those engaged in commerce. Men unloading ships, sailors, truck drivers, or in other words, working men."

Just as his helmet was about to be secured, the large man asked a final question.

"So, is that what all the teams are doin' today? Hittin' business targets?"

As the preparations for that morning's attack continued, Henson paused to stare at the big man. His eyes narrowing slightly, he said;

"You seem to be asking an awful lot of questions this morning, Thump. Tell me, why is that?"

"Well," the large man hesitated, much like a child asked why his hand was in the kitchen cookie jar. After only a short pause, though, he said, "it's like, with Carnahan gettin' himself taken out of the picture, I was ... well, kinda hopin' to show some initiative. Maybe move up a little." Henson considered the large man's answer, then nodded, smiling as he said;

"We'll see how you do today before we start talking promotions. But, an intelligent question deserves an answer. And that answer is no, the others are hitting some other kinds of targets. I'm not privy to the Boss's plans, but all three of the attacks this morning were designed to send different messages, and apparently to different people."

Henson shrugged absently, his face clearly showing he was perhaps a bit annoyed at not being told all the details of what was happening that morning. A quick glance at his watch, however, chased all personal thoughts from his mind. Noting the time, he announced;

"Gentlemen, it is eight fifty-five. Let's get moving. The Boss expects you on the street in five minutes. The truck picking you up will be here in twenty. The Boss is expecting a full fifteen minutes of slaughter. Let's give him his money's worth."

Several thugs cheered as the last of their metal gloves were sealed by technicians, or their bubble helmets were welded into place. As they had helped the thugs into their suits, their assistants had explained the importance of their energy packs, and the power lines leading from those packs to their weapons. They were also informed that they did not have to worry about recoil, since their weapons did not project force.

"Just point and shoot," one of the men in the smocks had said, "it's as easy as that."

And, with those words, at eight fifty-eight in the morning, the nine armored figures started for the doorway, each and every one of them prepared to begin killing as soon as they reached the outside. All except, that is, the large man who, as the group came close to the hallway leading to the outside, suddenly armed his weapon, and then fired upon the other eight!

23

THE ACCURSED LIGHT weapon had indeed been altered since last it had been used against the city. The first thing the big man noted was that its beam's color had shifted to a sinister, crackling orange, one shot through with dazzling sparks of red and yellow. The second thing he noted was that the beam, although it had a devastating effect on the walls, floor and ceiling of the hallway, had no effect whatsoever on the eight armored figures upon whom the large man had fired.

"Thump, what in hell're you doin'?"

The electronic voice was that of Hickey, the large man's friend. All the armored suits' helmets were interconnected through a series of miniaturized radios so their operators could communicate with one another, as well as their leaders. Before the big man, or anyone else could comment, however, Henson's voice came over the helmet's linked speakers, saying;

"I don't believe you're going to get an answer to your question, Hickey. Because I don't believe that is Thump you're speaking to."

The big man kept his finger on the trigger of his weapon, praying that continued firing might have some sort of cumulative effect. Dazzling orange splayed forth, filling the hallway, splattering mainly against the two closest of the other armored figures. Despite the increased rate of fire, however, the metal suits seemed impervious to the Accursed Light.

"Who are you?" Henson's voice came through the speakers once more. Remarkably calm, he said, "Tell us, and things might go easier on you."

"I'll tell you something," snarled the big man, his voice shifting in tone, deepening—becoming suddenly far more cultured. "There is no room in this world anymore for scum like you!"

"Gentlemen," came Henson's voice, "clearly we have an intruder. As you can see, your armor has been treated so one of you can not accidentally harm another. You can not hurt this man with your weapons any more than he can hurt you. There are other ways to incapacitate a man, however."

"I know a few of them," came the voice of the jokester from earlier. Immediately, Henson's voice returned, ordering;

"Very well, prove it. Three of you, subdue him. Take him alive if possible. If not—kill him. The rest, head outside. Complete your assignment. Go!"

As the five closest to the door continued on toward the outside, the others, including Hickey, turned to take down the imposter. As they drew closer, their target announced;

"Listen to me. My name is Richard Wentworth. I am a civilian commissioned by the governor to work with police throughout the state. This building is surrounded. Surrender to me, and I promise you will all live."

For a moment, two of the thugs hesitated. Wentworth's voice held such power, such raw authority, for a handful of seconds they found themselves suddenly unsure as to how they should proceed. Hickey, however, angry over having been somehow deceived by the imposter before him, snarled;

"Screw this bastard. He's lyin', lookin' to save his own skin. Let's take him."

Setting aside their weapons, the jokester and Hickey rushed Wentworth. At least, they did their best to do so in the heavy armored suits. Prepared, the criminologist lifted one leg and rammed it into the mid-section of the first thug to reach him. The man stumbled backward, arms flailing, unable to retain his balance. As he went down, slamming against the floor, Hickey backed up, suddenly not as certain as he had been seconds earlier of what to do next.

As for Wentworth, ever since his first attempt to stop the armored thugs had failed, he had been slowly retreating back into the main area of the warehouse. In the close quarters of the hallway, he knew he stood little chance of triumphing over the trio assigned to bring him down. Before he could move out of the line of fire, however, Hickey announced what the criminologist had already deduced.

"Hey, you know, maybe these things can't kill him outright, but when he was shootin' at us before, my suit was gettin' pretty hot. My guess is, if all three of us hit him with our beams, we can cook the bastard."

Without hesitation the trio of thugs turned their weapons on Wentworth, all of them bathing his armor in the deadly orange ray. As Hickey had predicted, the criminologist's armor began to warm significantly as the three beams washed over him.

"That's it," screamed Hickey, his voice raw with hate, "give him more. Give him all you got!"

All around the four, the walls of the hallway began to char. Great black gashes were burned into the building wherever the devastating beams touch down. Indeed, only seconds after their attack commenced, the ceiling burst into flames, its plaster melting, the resin in the cheap pine support beams boiling, then catching fire.

Inside his armor, Wentworth found himself sweating profusely. He blinked at the beads rolling down his forehead and into his eyes, cursing the bolted and welded helmet and gloves which kept him from wiping it from his eyes. Feeling his skin starting to bake, his lungs beginning to strain against the building heat frying his oxygen supply, the criminologist knew he had but seconds to extract himself from the jaws of death slowly closing about him.

"Think," he told himself. "You're supposed to be so smart, well now you'd better hurry up and prove it!"

And then, as sudden inspiration struck him, Wentworth stopped retreating, and instead threw himself forward at Hickey, pushing his way through the deadly orange light. His unexpected move caught all three of his enemies off-guard, giving him a handful of precious seconds to act. Taking his own rifle, Wentworth jammed it in roughly between the tank supplying Hickey's weapon and the shorter man's back. Without stopping, he then threw all his strength into wedging the tank free.

"What're you doin'," screamed Hickey, panic seizing him as he felt the wrenching strain running throughout his armor. "Get away from me, you freak!"

Wentworth only response was to apply more pressure. He could feel his weapon bending as he did so, suffered from the swelling temperature inside his own suit, but he continued on nevertheless, straining, throwing all his strength into his desperate move, until suddenly he stumbled as the tank tore loose from Hickey's armor. As the heavy container slammed against the cement floor, the criminologist pulled his weapon upward and then jammed it into the crack created in Hickey's suit.

"Oh God," squealed the thug, his voice cracking, filling with fear, "please—don't do it!"

Without hesitation, Wentworth pulled his trigger, sending the horrid orange energy burning through Hickey's suit. The thug screamed as the skin on his back crisped, as his flesh burst into flame, as his spine melted. Then, as a dark and putrid smoke began to slither forth through various seams in his armor, the smaller man went silent, his metal-encased corpse falling forward, slamming against the ground.

Without a word, the other two thugs moved forward on Wentworth. Both knew there was no escape for them if the intruder was not eliminated. He claimed to be with the police. That their forces were outside at that moment. Knowing their only chance was to murder Wentworth and then to perhaps somehow disappear back into the warehouse, they turned their weapons upon the criminologist a second time, hoping Hickey's plan might save them.

Inside his once more heating armor, Wentworth choked as the rising temperature grew ever more stifling. Dripping in sweat, barely able to see, the criminologist struck on one last desperate plan. Falling to his knees, he allowed the remaining two thugs to continue to bath him in the Accursed Light, even as he dragged Hickey's roasted carcass toward himself.

Smelling smoke, realizing his clothing was beginning to smoulder where it was coming into contact with his armor, Wentworth grabbed Hickey's rifle, jerking it savagely from the dead man's fingers. Then, grasping it in both hands, he twisted it violently and slammed it against the floor, managing to separate the rifle's butt from the hose leading to Hickey's back pack. Without hesitation Wentworth shoved the dead man into his companions, then staggered back to his feet.

The two remaining thugs side-stepped, allowing the body to fall in between them. Both stopped firing as they did so, each of them clever enough to realize what Wentworth was attempting. Some sort of a bluish-green liquid was spewing forth from the ruptured hose hanging from Hickey's tank. Staring for just an instant, not knowing exactly what might happen, but understanding that they were in trouble, both men turned and fled toward the outside.

Without hesitation, Richard Wentworth raised his weapon and fired directly into the puddle of fuel expanding across the floor, hoping for the best as the resulting explosion tossed his armored body backward as if he were the slightest of dolls!

24

OUTSIDE the warehouse on the lower west side's meat packing district, all eyes turned toward the structure as its front door was blown free, a massive billow of flame and smoke sending it flying some seventy yards, the door's jamb, and much of the front wall accompanying it. The door struck no one, but several large sections of flaming debris slammed against one of the armored thug, striking him with such force as to kill him instantly.

"Keep firing, men!"

The police lieutenant first to gather his wits could not be heard by all the officers in the area, but it mattered not. As those closest to the lieutenant opened fire, all of the others soon remembered why they were there, as did the thugs themselves. Both sides of the war returned to their small, but devastating, battle, neither certain of the outcome ahead.

At first, the armored criminals scoffed when they exited the warehouse to find themselves facing dozens of heavily armed policemen. They had been told their metal suits had been rendered impervious to bullets, and thus were not worried. Fearlessly standing in the open, they had brought the Accursed Light to bear on the officers, slaughtering many in the first few moments of their confrontation.

But, after a few minutes, the thugs began to discover a painful truth. Yes, their armor was bullet-proof. But only to a point. And, only against certain bullets. Not knowing what they were to face, but knowing that the warehouse they had been ordered to surround might unleash any of the scores of hideous weapons the New York City police department had faced over the years, those sent forth had decided to take no chances.

The officers assigned to the warehouse raid that morning were not sent with their standard .38 sidearms and nightsticks. They had been issued machine guns, many of them loaded with armor-piercing rounds. Brooklyn's Fort Hamilton had supplied the police with crates of grenades, as well as two mounted machine guns, the ammunition of which could pierce the armor of any vehicles outside of tanks.

By the time Wentworth's explosion tore the roof off the warehouse, two of the five armored thugs were already down for the count. The metal suit of one of them was so riddled with holes no one doubted he was dead. The other might have survived, but he remained so still none of the officers in the area were bothering to shoot at him any longer. Noting this, the last of the armored criminals threw down his weapon and raised his hands in the air. There would be no escape he knew, but he might possibly live.

At the same time, another armored figure staggered forth from the flaming debris of the warehouse. Realizing that he was holding no weapon, the police cautiously allowed him to approach. Then, when he crossed his arms at the wrist, holding them up in the air, the lieutenant in charge shouted;

"Hold your fire, men. It's Wentworth!"

DURING the next few minutes the police swarmed over the warehouse, daring to enter it from the rear and even to descend through skylights where the building was not yet in flames, in an attempt to capture as many of the gang as possible. As far as the officers on the lower west side were concerned, Richard Wentworth was a genius, and an incredibly brave one at that.

Assuring Kirkpatrick he could gain entry to the warehouse, he had left the commissioner with a powerful radio receiver, one tuned to pick up transmissions from a specially designed transmitter disguised as a wrist watch. Wentworth's plan was to enter the warehouse, transmit as much of the gang's plans as he could to the police outside, and then to help them in any way possible to stop whatever the latest threat turned out to be.

Realizing the threat of the gang having informants within the police force was all too possible, Kirkpatrick had worked through those officers he trusted implicitly, keeping the majority of the force completely in the dark as to what they were doing. Also, insisting his men have some means of identifying his friend, it was decided that an "X" would be Wentworth's means of revealing himself to the police. Thus crossing his arms had brought immediate recognition and saved him any further injury.

As soon as tools had been found so that his helmet could be removed, the criminologist asked what other sites had been attacked. The lieutenant in charge told him;

"Sorry, sir, but I don't have that information yet. We've been kind of busy. If you'd like to get out of the rest of that tin can, though, I can find out for you."

Nodding absently as he thanked the officer, Wentworth coughed, his throat dry and raspy from the intense heat he had suffered through inside the warehouse. After he had been blown backward by the explosion, he had lain dazed for a short time, nearly rendered unconscious. When he was able to rise, he found the building around him in flames. His weapon destroyed, Henson and his technicians nowhere to be seen, he had staggered toward the opening his battle with the trio of armored thugs had blown through the front of the building.

Battered and bruised, struggling to remain conscious after the devastating blow he had taken to the head, Wentworth wished he could sit down. Ironically, however, to escape the armor which had saved him from the explosion, he needed to remain upright so it could be removed from his body. Insisting the officers working on it strip away his gloves first, he then worked at removing the smeared and melted make-up which had allowed him to convince the gang that he was the late Robert Johnson.

Seared to his face as it was in some places, it felt good removing it simply for the physical relief. From the standpoint that what he was removing was the face of a thief and murderer, he was as anxious to have every vestige of it stripped from his person as he was the armor suit which still burned him in some spots. By the time the officers working on his armor had managed to remove all but the metal segments still encasing his legs and feet, the lieutenant had returned. He face did not show any indications that he might be bringing good news.

"What is it, officer? Where did they strike?"

"The bastards," growled the lieutenant, slamming his fist against his palm, his eyes burning with anger. "Filthy, miserable bastards!"

Growing concerned, Wentworth could not help but sigh with relief as the left boot of his armor was unbolted. Still, a growing dread replacing his curiosity, he asked;

"What is it, man? What have they done?"

"St. Peter's Cathedral," the lieutenant answered, his voice grim as death. "They slaughtered those attending morning services. They don't know how many are dead. Hundreds. Including the archbishop."

Wentworth was stunned. Yes, he had expected the gang to strike something completely different than a business site. Had considered they might strike a school. But a church, and not just a simple house of worship, but one designed to be an enduring monument to not only faith, but to art and beauty as well. The structure, a world-famous landmark, had now been turned into a mausoleum.

Shaking his head, wondering if there were any limits to the obscene horrors the Boss was ready to unleash upon his city, Wentworth gave the lieutenant a moment to catch his breath, then asked;

"They were to hit two targets besides this area. What was the other one?"

Looking Wentworth in the eye, having no idea how personally horrifying what he was about to say would be for the criminologist, the officer told him;

"They hit a hospital. Murdered hundreds more ... at least hundreds."

"A hospital?" His blood freezing, his mind exploding, eyes staring, throbbing, he shouted, "Which hospital?!"

"St. Christopher's."

25

THE NINE armored figures had torn through the hospital, killing all they could find, practically without opposition. This is not to say that many members of the staff of St. Christopher's did not try to prevent the massacre from taking place. Many of the doctors, janitors, interns, even nurses, made some kind of attempt to stop the metal-clad figures.

But, to no avail.

The Accursed Light acted as practically a scythe. The fragile commodity known as flesh held no ability to turn it aside. On floor after floor, sinister, crackling orange beams shot through with dazzling sparks of red and yellow filled the air with screams all too abruptly cut off, and coated the floors with lakes of blood which seemed to go on forever. Room after room, bed after bed—men, women or children—everyone that could be found was murdered without hesitation.

"Turn it up, you monkeys," snarled a thug by the name of Goodell. "We got a schedule to keep."

Goodell had been chosen to lead the team assaulting St. Christopher's because of his singular ability to ruthlessly focus upon a task. As the Boss saw it, in the past more than one villainous scheme had been brought low, at least in part, by the inferior mentality of the brutes employed to carry them out. Thinking only of their eventual rewards, caught up in the sudden power to found within their weapons, often such men were defeated simply by their inability to concentrate on their work. Goodell did not have such a problem.

He staggered his forces, kept them moving, his voice echoing through their helmets relentlessly, making certain they remembered their overall purpose. In and out— fifteen minutes. Goodell allowed his force to kill as many patients and caretakers as they liked—that was part of their assignment, after all—as long as they did not linger.

"This is the floor," the team leader shouted, making certain the trio he had brought with him all realized the fact. "So let's get this done."

As the first two armored men exited the elevator, a score of bullets ricocheted uselessly from their suits. The half-dozen police officers present—some assigned to guard Commissioner Kirkpatrick, others there simply by chance— had blocked the hallway with tables, chairs, gurneys, anything they could find, and then taken shelter behind it so they could stand against the invaders. None of their effort proved to be in any way effective.

Coldly, laughing as they did so, the thugs in the lead aimed their weapons and played the Accursed Light over the blockade before them. Men died screaming, limbs cut from their bodies, torsoes sliced in half. Their quite solid defensive line offered them no protection. The orange beams dissolved both wood and metal, punching through almost immediately to slaughter the policemen making their valiant, if futile, stand.

"All those cops being here *proves* this is where we

want to be," snapped Goodell. Glancing at the time piece build into the inside of his helmet, knowing they had to vacate the hospital soon, he added;

"Find Kirkpatrick. Finish him. Then, get the girl."

The pair broadcast their assurance they would find and finish both their targets in seconds as they moved forward toward the now flaming barrier. Without hesitation, the larger of the two slung his rifle into its holster, then turned his attention to the burning wall. Trusting his armor, the thug threw his shoulder against the center of the barrier and smashed his way through almost without effort. Turning to his companions he waved them on as he shouted;

"See ... nuthin' to it."

But, immediately after he spoke, as his fellows watched, suddenly his armored form moved awkwardly, shuffling sideways as if somehow he had lost his balance. As those on the other side of the blazing wall watched, their companion's arms reached helplessly for his weapon. His hands slapped against it several times, but for some reason his fingers did not seem capable of closing around its stock. Before either Goodell or the fellow with him could comment, the lead thug finally simply dropped to his knees, tumbling backward into the flames.

And then, the others' questions were answered.

"More of you," thundered Ram Singh's voice, a burst of eager anticipation running through it, "ahhhh, so very good. Hell needs all the meat it can find."

For a moment Goodell merely stared, scarcely able to comprehend the sight before him. Standing in between the two blazing stacks of furniture was a man—one armed with only a sword. His mind racing, sections of it screaming that what he was seeing could not be, the leader of the assault team worked desperately to get himself moving once more.

Yes, he reminded himself, their armor was bulletproof. Yes, it could not even be harmed by the Accursed Light itself. But, in their pride over the destructive qualities of their weapons, and in the supposed invulnerability of their suits, those who had created them had overlooked the fact that while their armor could easily turn a blunt projectile, its joints could be breached by a well-placed blade.

"Still, what does it matter," Goodell whispered smugly. "Whoever that jackass is, he can't reach us from over there, but we can reach *him*!"

Without hesitation, the thug brought his rifle up and fired, stabbing its beam through the opening in the blazing wall. As Singh dodged to the left, Goodell compensated, wrenching his weapon in the same direction. Savagely, he splashed the deadly light against the flaming barrier, as well as the floor and ceiling. His beam had sliced through much of the hastily assembled furniture, but Goodell had no idea if it had reached his foe. With the hall filling with smoke, and time growing short, he pointed toward the man with him and ordered;

"Get that crazy turbaned son of a bitch. I'll get Kolwalski. We've got to finish and get the hell out of here."

The other thug moved forward, firing his weapon through the left side of the barrier as had his team leader, reducing it to burning scraps. Supremely confident only seconds earlier, the man's god-like notions had suddenly evaporated. He had entered St. Christopher's with an overwhelming confidence, certain he could destroy anything without fear. Moving throughout the hospital, he had laughed as he had turned his beam on those he had found in their beds, cackled with glee as he had watched their hair burst into flames, their eyes melt. He had taken a particular glee in bringing the glowing hell to children.

But now, the fun of the moment had been ruined. Suddenly, his euphoria had been shattered by some maniac with a sword—a sword, of all things—some miserable lunatic who had dared defy their power. Flooding the left side of the hall with the Accursed Light, he moved forward into the building smoke, screaming;

"You're dead, you hear me, asshole? You're *dead!*"

Smashing through what little remained of the left hand side of the barrier, the thug peppered the darkly cloudy area before him with the Accursed Light, burning the floor, scorching the walls, and laughing all the while, until the moment when Ram Singh's sword tore through his right armpit.

As the man's screams filled Goodell's helmet, the Sikh made certain his blade's edge was aimed downward. Then, as he had with his first victim, he sliced downward along the armor's seam. He was only able to force his powerful sword a half a foot down through the armor. By angling his blade, he tore through the thug's lungs and heart, killing him with that single stroke.

Goodell stood for a second, his eyes wide, unblinking, slowly comprehending what the Sikh had done. He had allowed them to observe him moving to the left, then had obviously doubled back, rolling across the floor, using the still intact bottom of the barrier as well as the smoke building there in the hallway to cover his move.

"Two of us," he thought, his forehead beginning to perspire. "Two of us—stopped by ... a sword."

Enraged, Goodell screamed for the last of his men there with him to attack. As the other man moved forward, slowly—cautiously—the team leader debated what he should do. They had found neither Kirkpatrick nor the girl. The truck coming to pick them up would be arriving soon—according to the time piece in his helmet, in less than two minutes.

Following his man forward, Goodell radioed the others, telling them to head for the truck. He told them that he and Kolwalski would accomplish their main goal in seconds and then follow them out. Giving the others a final instruction to try and get the truck's driver to wait for them, he then turned his full attention to the problem before him.

Focusing on that problem Goodell radioed Kolwalski, telling him to stop for a moment. Conferring via their radios, the two thugs agreed neither of them could see any trace of the swordsman. The hallway was thick with smoke at that point. Suddenly spotting the number on a door which the hospital records had listed as being Kirkpatrick's room, Goodell snapped his weapon around and fired.

Blasting the door, slicing through the walls, the thug poured all the power he could squeeze from his weapon. Above all, their assignment had been to kill the commissioner. The sinister orange beam carved plaster, wood and mesh like soft cheese, utterly destroying the room, slicing through the outside wall to send a shower of glass and brick plummeting to the street below.

As his second joined him, adding his beam to Goodell's, after only a moment the entire area shook as the floor and a vast section of several walls collapsed, crashing downward into the room below. Shouting into his radio, the team leader announced;

"Good enough! One outta two ain't bad. The commissioner was the big target. Now let's just get out of here."

Both men turned to head back for the stairwell, when

both were hit by a white splash. Something had been thrown at their helmets, something red and thick. Something which had suddenly rendered both of them blind.

Goodell cursed in confusion, then suddenly screamed as a sharp pain tore through the back of his knee. Blind, not knowing where his assailant was, not caring, he pulled his weapon around and fired in all directions as he slammed against the floor. Or, at least, he tried to do so.

He did not succeed.

Observing the armored thugs as they had first approached, Ram Singh had spotted their obvious weakness—their helmets. As the police officers with him had unleashed their first, futile volley, he had searched frantically for something with which to blind their enemies. Finding several bottles of blood, he had slid them into the massive pockets of his breeches and vest. Then, when given a clear chance, he had used them.

Goodell had gone down after the Sikh had sliced through the joint at the back of the thug's knee. As he screamed in pain, the group leader pulled the trigger on his weapon a dozen times, waving it in every direction as he did so. It was of no use to him, however, for Singh had already sliced through the tube connecting his rifle to his backpack.

"Kolwalski," he screamed. "Kill this son of a bitch! Do it—*do it!*"

Goodell's order came too late. The last of his men already lay dead on the smoldering floor next to him, his heart pierced, furiously spraying the inside of his armor with blood. And, as for Goodell himself, the last of the armored thugs had only a handful of seconds to wonder what was happening beyond his scarlet-stained helmet before he heard the sound of a finely-honed blade tearing at its neck seam.

26

"**I** GRIEVE to tell you this, Sahib, but I must." Ram Singh's voice quavered, its tone stuck between sorrow and anger. Holding his employer by the shoulders, staring him directly in the eye, he hesitated for only a second longer, then said;

"Both Stanley Kirkpatrick *and* Miss Nita ... are dead."

Wentworth made no reply. He uttered no sound, made no gesture. Standing stock still in the midst of the utter pandemonium outside St. Christopher's, he looked to all the world like a man not merely in shock, but one who had died and simply had not yet fallen over. He was surrounded by reporters from every radio outlet and newspaper, but none of them questioned him. There were limits to such intrusions. Several photographers snapped pictures, most notably the one sent by *The City Bugle*. Even he stopped, however, when he noted the grim looks of disgust being thrown at him by his peers.

"Take ... take me home."

Slowly Ram Singh guided his employer back to the car in which he had arrived. Helping him into the back seat, the Sikh shut the door quietly, then raced around to the driver's door. He paused for a moment before entering, needing a moment to cough violently. He had inhaled a great deal of smoke during his battle with the armored thugs, and for a moment experienced a wave of nauseating dizziness. Shaking it off, however, he slid inside the roadster and then gunned its powerful engine. Seconds later he was weaving his way carefully through the ever-growing crowd of police, media, and the curious.

The vehicle and its occupants were hardly missed. The

crowd had enough to occupy itself. After all, the Accursed Light had returned to the city. It had been unleashed at the docks. It had murdered hundreds at St. Peter Cathedral. Hundreds more at St. Christopher's Memorial Hospital. Hundreds and hundreds more to add to the roster of the dead. Including, the archbishop of New York, Police Commissioner Kirkpatrick—

And socialite Nita Van Sloan.

"SO, SAHIB, do you see my future fortunes taking me to Broadway?"

"Well, I think we convinced the vultures, but I wouldn't quit your day job."

Wentworth sat back, resting his head against the seat, closing his eyes. It would take Singh at least twenty minutes to return them to Sutton Place and he needed that time to think.

Knowing that the criminologist would head directly for the hospital once he heard of the attack, Ram Singh had moved quickly. Prying open Goodell's helmet, he had bounced the criminal's head off the floor several times, after which he began applying pressure to the man's eyes with his thumbs. In but seconds, the bleeding, frightened Goodell has admitted that Kirkpatrick and Nita were the main targets of their attack.

Leaving him screaming on the smoking floor, the Sikh had found Sergeant Thomas Carpenter, an officer he knew both Kirkpatrick and Wentworth felt was above any suspicion, and told him what he had learned. Quickly they had gathered a few of the other officers Carpenter knew the commissioner trusted, and they had moved Kirkpatrick and the still unconscious Nita to ambulances supposedly leaving for St. Christopher's sister hospital.

Then, Singh had used a police radio to contact Wentworth. He knew, of course, that all their vehicles were equipped to monitor police frequencies, and that his employer would not only be on his way to the hospital if at all possible, but that he would be tuned in listening for any information. After he had explained what he had done, the Sikh and Wentworth planned how they would proceed.

Their plan was simple. Wentworth would receive the terrible news from his loyal servant, and then go into seclusion. Carpenter would release an "official" statement, letting everyone know that both Kirkpatrick and Nita had been sliced into nearly unrecognizable pieces by the Accursed Light. In the meantime, they would both be removed to Sutton Place. As would another.

Certain his home was being watched, the ambulances would not drive directly to the mansion, but rather to a spot on the next block where its passengers would be disembarked and then transported to Wentworth's home through a hidden tunnel. Jenkyns was instructed to inform Kirkpatrick's wife of what had happened, but also to tell her for her own good as well as his, that she should remain at home and play the grieving widow. He also assured her that the commissioner would call her as soon as he was safely ensconced.

Jackson, in the meantime, was ordered to bring in a team of doctors and nurses willing to live at Sutton Place for the duration so both the new arrivals would have all the care they might need. After that he was to double the guards already in place.

"Bringing in more security shouldn't look suspicious," thought Wentworth. "With Nita targeted by them, it's obvious someone is sending me a message. Why wouldn't I protect myself?" Staring out the window, watching the crosstown blocks roll by, he asked himself;

"Now, all I have to figure out is what message I was being sent. And by whom."

IN LESS that two hours, all Wentworth had thrown into motion had been accomplished. Nita, still unconscious, had been moved into her own rooms. Her attending physician had examined her thoroughly, and while his news was not encouraging, at least she was still holding her own.

Ruthlessly, Wentworth pushed all thoughts of his beloved from his mind. What would happen to Nita next was beyond his control. All he could do would be to protect her from further harm. And, he knew, the best way to do that was to find the Boss, and destroy his gang once and for all. Sitting in his study, he was just about to contact Jenkyns to inquire as to how Kirkpatrick was doing when the door opened, and the commissioner was wheeled in by Ram Singh. Guiding Kirkpatrick's chair to the front of Wentworth's desk, the Sikh announced;

"You have a most insistent visitor, Sahib."

"Your timing couldn't be more perfect. Can I offer you a Scotch, Stanley?"

"Can you? What in blazes took you so long?"

Wentworth dispatched Singh to both task Jenkyns with putting together a meal for himself and the commissioner and gather some glasses, ice, and the best Scotch in the house. While they waited for both, the criminologist said;

"Well, where do we begin?"

"At this point, I must admit that I am eminently open to suggestions."

As Singh returned with a silver tray containing a large ice bucket, two sturdy cut crystal tumblers, and a rather exquisite decanter filled with a sweetly amber-colored liquid which made Kirkpatrick smack his lips, Wentworth inquired;

"Has Sergeant Carpenter arrived yet?"

"He called some five minutes ago," answered the Sikh, already filling the tumblers with ice, "basically to let us know he would be doing so at any time now. Since we were only able to secure two ambulances at the hospital without arousing suspicion, one of those had to return for him ... and our other guest."

Noting the wicked smile curling across Singh's face, the commissioner accepted the glass he was being handed, asking at the same time;

"Our *other* guest?"

"A most talkative fellow I met at St. Christopher's," answered the Sikh innocently.

"Talkative, you say?"

"Oh my, yes, commissioner," added Singh, his tone still as guileless as possible.

"Good," growled Kirkpatrick. Taking a long pull of his drink, knowing his doctor would scream bloody murder if he saw him doing so, he smacked his lips in appreciation, then said;

"And ... you'll be here when Carpenter gets here ... to help keep this fellow ... talkative. Right, Singh?"

"Oh, it will be my very great pleasure, sir."

The three men all looked at one another for a moment, each of them understanding exactly what was coming. None of the trio felt the slightest hesitation toward what they would be doing next. If anything, they were looking forward to it.

27

THE questioning of Goodell did not prove to take very much time at all. Like so many of his ilk, the thug proved to be the worst kind of coward. Unable to decide if he were more frightened by being in the hands of the police, or within the grasp of Ram Singh once more, what little the low-level gang leader knew of the Boss and his plans, Goodell fearfully revealed in exacting detail. But, unlike Thump before him, being somewhat higher within the organization, Goodell knew a few more useful things than his predecessor.

The first fact he confirmed was that the city was indeed in for two more days of brutal attacks. He had no idea what the next day held, however. Goodell explained that the Boss was careful not to assign men to perform two missions in a row simply because if this or that henchmen were killed or captured, that meant his schedule might be jeopardized. Since Goodell was scheduled to be one of the support people for the third day's attack, however, he did know much of it details and revealed everything he knew to his inquisitors.

The next day, New York was plagued by a device named the Dissolver by the first to use it years earlier, a hideous salt which literally melted the flesh from its victim's body. The Boss made the next day's murder spree even more spectacular than any of those previous by sending forth ten squads of killers. The escalation in numbers certainly terrified many, but it was not the Boss's master stroke. What allowed the Boss to once more catch the police off guard was that for the first time, none of the attacks took place within Manhattan.

Two of the Boss's teams struck on Staten Island, two in the Bronx, three in Queens and three in Brooklyn. Eyewitness reports, when studied together, revealed a consistent pattern. In each of that day's massacres, a team consisting of five men would surround a large, open public area, and then slaughter everyone they could, driving their victims in toward the center of the chosen site. The estimates of the dead by day's end totaled more that three thousand.

The next day, however, the authorities were somewhat prepared, for Goodell could tell them much about what to expect. On that day the Boss planned to release a force of mechanical men. When used in the past the fire-spitting dreadnoughts had been controlled by men who entered the gigantic mechanisms and piloted them from inside. The Boss, more interested, it seemed, in terror than profit, had tasked those working for him with transforming the murder machines into independent robots.

Fifteen of the deadly automatons were to be unleashed during the morning rush hour and Goodell knew to what sites four of them were to be delivered. His information proved accurate, and that quartet was met by dedicated police officers armed with high powered machine guns, explosives and small cannons. That group caused little trouble for anyone. The remaining eleven robots were able to perpetrate considerable mayhem, however, giving the radio commentators, and newspapers like the muck-raking *City Bugle*, more ammunition with which to terrorize the citizens of New York City.

Richard Wentworth did not leave Sutton Place during the fifth and sixth attacks. He had been badly slammed about during his struggle against the Accursed Light, one which had aggravated some of his older wounds. His driving concern for Nita had kept him moving far longer than any other man could have endured. However, once he had reached the protective security of his home, and had seen his beloved safely ensconced within its boundaries, the criminologist had finally given in to his wounds and allowed himself to take some rest.

He did so for more than the obvious reason that he could scarcely do otherwise. Wentworth was a man used to pushing himself far beyond the limits of mortal endurance. He could have returned to the streets to take up arms against the Dissolver and the mechanical men. But, that would have been thinking like a foot soldier, and not a general, and a leader is what New York needed at that moment.

As far as the world knew, both his fiancée and best friend had just died. Staying home grieving was good protective cover at that moment. Also, he needed to be there for the questioning of Goodell. Both he and Kirkpatrick had been through debilitating ordeals. Between the two of them they had been able to wring as much information as possible. Working through trusted officers like Carpenter, the pair had been able to orchestrate the defense of the city between them. They had also been able to continue several lines of investigation into the nature of the Boss's organization, as well as the mysterious leader's identity.

Beyond that, Wentworth had another reason for remaining at Sutton Place. A personal reason.

Nita.

Nita, who lay dying within the walls of his home. Nita, who meant more to him than anything in the world. Nita, whose side from which he found it nearly impossible to tear himself away. In earlier times he had left her behind more than once in such a state to roar forth once more against the forces of evil. This time, however, with no clear target, with no clues as to where his enemy might lurk, for once he had allowed himself the simple luxury of concern. Needing rest himself, he had allowed himself respite while watching over her. He would leave her side to confer with Kirkpatrick, to help outline strategies with Carpenter, to check the defenses of Sutton Place, et cetera. But always, he would return. Always, he would be once more at her side, staring at her broken, fragile body.

Hour after hour, minute by minute, his strength returned to him as his growing despair inflamed the anger within him, fanning it like a bellows, intensifying his rage to a blinding white heat. By the evening of the day which had brought the return of the mechanical men, Richard Wentworth was as rested as he needed to be. Any other man might have required weeks more of convalescence, but they were not he.

Studying the reports of the day's slaughter, Wentworth, Kirkpatrick and Carpenter sat in the criminologist's office, preparing to make their next move. If the Boss held to his pattern, they would have three days of rest with which to intensify their search for him. Pulling at his chin, Wentworth mused;

"But, why would he do so?"

"What do you mean, sir?"

"Well, think about it, Carpenter. This 'Boss' has kept us off our guard by continually doing the unexpected. All we know for certain is that he wants New York terrified—"

"And," Kirkpatrick cut his friend off, "if the city expects three days of quiet, and the ceiling fell in once more ... all the terror one could wish for."

The trio did not debate the notion. Once presented, nothing else made more sense. But, sadly they had no where to take the idea. Ram Singh's capture of Goodell had been most fortuitous, in that it had allowed them to save a great many lives. But, those names and addresses he could give them had led to nothing more than the disruption of a few of the Boss's cells. His operation had not been crippled in any significant manner. His identity had not been revealed.

Worse, Goodell had been the only one of the Boss's men captured alive who possessed any useable information at all. The police had been able to bring down a few others during the fifth attack, but they had been foot soldiers only. Possessing of no useful knowledge. Useless. And, as for the sixth attack, even though all the murder machines had been stopped, it was not as if they could question robots for information.

As the three sat in their chairs, Kirkpatrick smoking a cigar absently, not really tasting it, Carpenter sipping at yet another cup of coffee, Wentworth pulled out a stack of notes he had made at the beginning of the entire affair, determined to examine every bit of evidence they had once more. When he got to the envelope of photographs given them by Basilton of the Bugle, he stopped.

Holding the envelope in his hand, he stared at it, not so much actually looking at it, but using it to focus his will, to dredge his memory. What was it that nagged him so about the horrid collection of prints? The back of his mind had obviously not been satisfied about them on some level— but, he asked himself, what level could that be?

What was it he was trying to tell himself?

And then, as Wentworth searched his memory for whatever forgotten mote was troubling him so, suddenly Jenkyns entered, carrying a small package.

"This was just delivered for you gentlemen from police headquarters. I was informed that it is quite urgent you examine it immediately."

"More good news," joked Carpenter sourly.

"No, sir," answered the butler. "I was led to believe by those who delivered it that it was not."

28

THE package proved to contain a short, hand-written letter, accompanied by a single reel of magnetized plastic tape. The missive stated that the tape was what everyone had been waiting for since the latest series of attacks against the city had begun—a message from the Boss, one finally outlining what he wanted. The tape in the packet was not the original, but a copy of the one sent to police headquarters. It had been made and sent by those in the department who knew Kirkpatrick was still alive.

They advised that the commissioner listen to it as quickly as possible. Apparently further copies of the tape had also been sent by the Boss to the newspapers and radio stations as well. And ... not just the local ones.

"Seems a little odd, don't it," asked Carpenter. "This guy's got a beef with New York. Why send tapes to radio stations in Chicago, or newspapers in Los Angeles?"

"Who knows," answered Wentworth. "I suppose to find out we'd best do as instructed here ... listen to it and discover the reason for ourselves."

So saying, the criminologist instructed Jenkyns to have Jackson fetch his tape recorder from the den and bring it to his office. Some fourteen minutes later, the five men gathered around the machine set up on Wentworth's desk. As the rest made themselves comfortable, Jenkyns started the device playing, and the five listened to the message sent from the Boss to the world.

"Attention, this most modest of communications

is hereby directed to the entire population of the world. Please understand, you are all, now, merely nothing more than my slaves. Regardless of what you might believe to the contrary, all personal freedoms are now completely and utterly rescinded. Those who obey shall be spared. Those who attempt defiance shall not."

Wentworth reached forth and turned the heavy toggle controlling the tape recorder's power to the "off" position for a moment. As he did so, he asked;

"Anyone recognize that voice?" When the others all announced they did not, the criminologist added that he concurred, but that they should keep possible identification in mind as they were listening, then switched the machine back on once more.

"I realize many have been wondering what we want. In all honesty a fair question. Why would someone do as we have done? Why so much murder and mayhem, why so much blood spilled without any demands? Why would a group put forth so much effort, expend so much energy, invest so much treasure, without looking for reward of one kind or another?"

"Yes," wondered Wentworth, his eyes fixed to the tape recorder in a harsh gaze as if the machine itself were his enemy, "why, indeed?"

"We have asked for no ransom, made no blackmail demands, of New York City, because we do not want anything more from New York City than we have already taken. This grand metropolis has been for us, merely a proving grounds, a sampler ... a showcase, as it were."

Although all those listening were putting effort into trying to determine the identity of the speaker, no one was straining harder to recognize the voice on the tape than Wentworth himself. The criminologist did not believe any attempt was being made by the boss to disguise his voice vocally, but rather that he was speaking through some sort of filtering device, possibly electronic in nature.

"Very clever," thought Wentworth, scowling as he did so, "unfortunately for us."

Master of disguise that he was, the criminologist knew how difficult it was for most people to actually change the tonal qualities of their speech so as to remain unrecognizable to those who knew them. There was something about the Boss's voice that was nagging at him, screaming out that Wentworth did know the person to whom he was listening. Determined to solve the riddle, he closed his eyes so as to intensify his powers of concentration as the Boss chuckled briefly, then continued, offering;

"Forgive me, but we have been so amused by those wondering what we wanted, when our demands would come, and so forth. Allow me to put the city treasury office at ease. We wish nothing from the grand City of New York. Not a single nickel. As I said, New York is merely our demonstration site for the world. It is the world that shall pay. It is you all that shall pay. But not in any fashion, I do believe, you might have expected."

"Sergeant Carpenter," said Kirkpatrick to the officer next to him, "I do believe we can start to worry now."

"Way ahead of you, chief."

Both Wentworth and Jackson grinned slightly at the gallows humor being displayed by the two policemen. Jenkyns, as always the perfect butler, did not allow any show of emotion. Before any further comments could be made, the Boss's voice issued once more from the recorder.

"Our planet has become a sorry state. You would think we, the population of the world, would have learned something during the Great War, as we called it then. Do you remember what we called it, in our naiveté, 'the war to end all wars?' That monstrous political folly which brought our current chaos down upon us. How quaint it all seems now.

"For my own purposes, however, I feel I really must thank the leaders of Europe who felt the need to punish Germany into submission. Their petty greed forged a national hatred in the Germanic peoples which gifted us with their ever-so-charming Chancellor Hitler. And now, now nearly all the nations of Earth have been stretched thin, weakened, left vulnerable. That, my dear slaves, is where we come in."

"I don't think I like where this is going, Richard." Giving Kirkpatrick a strained grin, Wentworth answered;

"Come now, Stanley, where's your sense of adventure?"

"The weapons you have seen unleashed so far," the electronic voice hissed on, "these are but a fraction of the terrors my organization has collected over the years. And, as those in the know have realized by now, although we've noted certain facts have been held back from the public, the defects these weapons held in the past have been eliminated. We are, right now, the most powerful force on the face of the planet. And, that being the case, it seems to us only fitting that we rule the planet."

"Funny how that kind of logic always appeals to guys like this," muttered Carpenter.

"Try, if you will, Parisians, to imagine your beloved Eiffel Tower a smoking ruin. Or cholera, ravaging the streets of Bombay, Stockholm, Chicago. Think of our fire robots, marching through Rome or Montreal. Contemplate waking up to the rolling sound of distant thunder, only to discover that Sydney, or Lima, or Washington D.C. had been blown off the face of the map."

"Who?" The question echoed within Wentworth's mind. "Who in the name of God is that speaking?"

Several qualities in the taped voice, even disguised as it was by some unknown combination of filters, were tearing at the criminologist's consciousness. He knew the speaker, was positive of it, and yet, he could not put his finger squarely on the Boss's identity.

"This is the world you will know, if all nations are not given over to us. Any nation which does not surrender its sovereign rights to us—utterly and completely—will know torment and death as it has never known before. The madness of world war will cease. All nations shall march forward into a new age hand in hand, together, with all men as brothers, for there shall no longer be any choice given to anyone in the matter.

"Like any parent, there comes a time when they must say 'no' to their unruly children and put an end to squabbling and bickering for the greater good. And so, you shall, all of you, all the peoples of the world, you shall all become our slaves, for only through this measure shall you all be made free."

"This person is a certifiable lunatic."

"At the least, Jenkyns," offered Jackson to the butler, scratching his head as he did so. Wentworth made no comment, however. The criminologist was concentrating, throwing the entirety of his great mental powers behind unraveling the secret of the Boss's identity.

"And, to prove to you all that this is no idol threat, we shall continue our destruction of the City of New York until nothing of it remains. Tomorrow we shall pull down its greatest symbol as a sign to all that we are deadly serious.

We do not do this with malice. But as always, some must be sacrificed for all to be saved. And, trust us, one and all, you shall be saved from yourselves.

"We do as we do for the greater good. Try to think of us as your benefactors. We truly do regret the necessity of destroying New York, but it must be done. An example had to be made. It is, after all, merely good business."

At that point, the voice on the tape went silent. In the office of Richard Wentworth, none spoke. Kirkpatrick, still in a wheelchair, had looked small and shrunken when first he had arrived at Sutton Place. Now, he looked as if all the life had been wrung from him, as if his heart had been torn from his chest and thrown to the dogs.

Jenkyns, so shocked had he been by the Boss's statements, had forgotten himself and sat down rather than remain in his normal rigid butlering stance. Jackson and Carpenter sat as well, both men silent, lost in the grim wave of hopelessness that had washed across the others.

But, behind his desk, Wentworth stared at the now silent, but still running tape recorder, his eyes suddenly growing wide. His mouth falling open, he began to chuckle, giddy with hope as his hand flashed forward to first stop the machine, then begin its rewinding process. As the others questioned him, he waved them all to silence, stopping the recording device once more, then setting it to play.

"... regret the necessity of destroying New York, but it must be done. An example had to be made. It is, after all, merely good business."

And then, Richard Wentworth slammed his fist against the desk as he threw his head back to laugh. The noise he made was loud and near hysterical, flat and mocking, and he howled it forth with glee, much to the amazement of the others. After only a few seconds indulgence, however, the criminologist contained himself and sat forward, staring at those around him with a wide, knowing grin filling his face as he announced;

"And now, my fine gentlemen, the holding action is over. Now, at last ... we fight back!"

29

"SO, DO you really think this is where the Boss is going to strike today?"

Ram Singh turned his head slightly toward Jackson, his eyes dark and solemn in the early morning gloom. The great Sikh sat cross-legged on the cold steel floor, running a well-used piece of whet-stone across the long curve of his sword. Without looking up from his work, he answered;

"Are you telling me that it is possible you doubt Sahib Richard's abilities to see through to the truth, after all these years? Truly?"

The two men sat in the slowly dissipating darkness, awaiting the attack the Boss had promised. Despite the fact they were not alone, both were still heavily armed as if expecting to have to face an entire army themselves.

"Hey, none of that. The major's done all right by me and how, and you know it." Jackson thought for a moment, then in a faraway voice, he added;

"And, I mean, he's been doing it for more years than I like to admit could have passed. Yeah, he's a genius, and there's no denying it. But still, thinking he knows who this nut case is just because of a single phrase ... I don't know ... I mean, that's a lot to ask just on faith."

Nodding unconsciously, Ram Singh lifted his eyes for a moment, sending them staring out over the calm waters of the Manhattan bay area before him. The pre-dawn gloom still too deep to be pierced, the Sikh returned to his work, answering quietly;

"Yes, it is." Rolling his shoulders slightly, making certain they were limber for the battle he was certain to come, Singh added;

"But tell me, my friend, how is that in any way different from that which he has asked from us all of our lives with him?"

At the same moment, Richard Wentworth found himself beyond the other end of his home island. Whereas Ram Singh and Jackson were just south of Manhattan, their employer was just north of it, outside the city entirely in the town of Yonkers. Whereas they had been in position for several hours, however, he had just finished parking his roadster in the shadows created by a copse of trees near his objective.

Judging the depth of the early morning gloom to be sufficient for his needs, he slipped quietly from his vehicle out into the early morning darkness, closing his car's door silently, working hard to remain undetected. He was, after all, in a very exclusive residential area, a place of sprawling mansions known for its genteel manner. The sight of the black-garbed crimefighter was not something to which the neighborhood he was prowling was very accustomed. Then again, how could any place grow accustomed to a presence such as the *Spider*?

"Well," he thought, studying the sprawling grounds before him, "this is it. Or at least, it had better be."

Standing in the breaking darkness outside the mansion in which he believed he would find the Boss, the *Spider* reminded himself that both Kirkpatrick and Jackson had not been as certain as he. Being honest, he also admitted to himself that they could not be faulted for doing so. He was, admittedly, working on the slimmest of assumptions.

Still, another part of his brain reminded him with a slight tinge of indignation, had he not done so with overwhelming success over the years? Constantly? Had his hunches not proved correct a thousand times, saved millions of lives? *Millions?*

"Yes, they have," he thought, then before he could congratulate himself, a further voice from the back of his mind added in a tone justly stark and severe;

"But you have been *wrong*, as well, have you not? And, more than merely wrong—you have convinced yourself of utter insanities. Do you remember, more than once, of believing Ram had turned against you? That Jackson and Jenkyns were spies for your enemies? Believing that Nita had betrayed you? *Nita?* No, you might be brilliant, but you are not always correct. You, sir, are not always right."

Wentworth hung his head for a moment, taking in a deep breath, holding it for a long, condemning handful of seconds before exhaling once more. It was true. The life he had chosen had driven him to utter madness on more than one occasion. The need to make instantaneous decisions, exercising the power of life and death, acting as judge, jury and executioner, and on no one's authority but his own—

"Yes," he told himself, "I remember. And that is why we've learned to think things through. I'm not basing my actions at this moment on mere speculation. I know something about voices, how to disguise them, what to look for when someone is attempting to do so. When your own life so often depends on such abilities, you learn what to watch for when others try to do the same in your presence. You listen for the patterns they forget to mask. You watch for signature phrases."

Confident, the *Spider* made what would appear to anyone else to be nothing more than a casual forward motion, one which had him against, up and over the mansion's twelve foot stone wall in seconds. Landing silently behind the modest stand of firs he had chosen to mask his entry, he let his eyes pass over the expansive lawn before him, adding with a bit of a smirk;

"Besides, if I'm wrong, and I do not find proof that the Boss lives here, I simply won't kill anyone."

Then, spotting three obvious sentries coming around the far left corner of the main house, all of them armored, all of them carrying the deadly orange-flame spitting rifles of the Accursed Light, he allowed himself a moment of self-satisfaction as he thought;

"But then again, in all our time, how often have we actually been wrong?"

Silently, the *Spider* glided over the soggy mid-March grounds, ready to put an end to the Boss's reign of fear and madness once and for all.

"SO, CARPENTER," Jackson spoke into his bulky Army hand radio, "you and your boys ready?"

"We've got four boats surrounding the island," replied the sergeant. "We've got you two as lookouts. As soon as you spot anything, we move in at whatever point you say. I'd say we're as ready as possible."

"Okay, don't get excited. After all, we just know the Boss is hitting this site sometime today. We've got a lot of hours left to go."

"Yeah, we've got hours," agreed the officer, "*if* it's actually this site."

"Yeah, okay," agreed Jackson sourly, "there is that part."

And then, Singh held up a hand, indicating he wished silence. Signing off, Jackson looked at the large Sikh with curiosity. The warrior's hand had stopped moving across his blade. Holding stock still, he had shut his eyes, turned his head sideways and appeared to be listening to something, or for something, his companion could not yet discern.

"What is it," whispered Jackson. His eyes still closed, Singh replied;

"Can you not hear it? Something approaches our position." The Sikh waited another moment, then his head straightened, his eyes opened wide, as he added;

"Something airborne."

As if to prove the large warrior's point, at that exact moment the dull hum which he had detected moments earlier became clear to Jackson as well.

"Something headed this way."

And then, as both men peered outward into the slowly lifting haze of morning, they saw the approaching airships, suddenly realized they had no means to stop them!

DECIDING the time for subtlety had passed, the *Spider* raced forward across the lawn, his cloak pulled tight around himself. He kept his body fast within the darkest line of shadow available to him, but he did not move slowly, did not try and mask the sound of his approach as his boots broke the slight crust of frost glazing the mansion's lawn. Having worn the Accursed Light armor himself so recently, he was well aware that one of its weaknesses was the fact that its helmets muffled outside sounds considerably.

Also, taking into consideration what Singh had told him about his own encounter with the armored thugs, the *Spider* had brought with him a weapon he did not normally carry. Bursting from his slight bit of cover, Wentworth

"Sure, but what're you going to do?"

"Make ready." Stopping for just a moment, Singh grinned, adding, "After all, if the police can not stop these most vulgar of assassins, then the glory for doing so will simply have to fall to another."

Before Jackson could reply, the massive Sikh disappeared into the darkness of the statue's steel interior.

MUCH to the surprise of those watching from their remote viewing area, the *Spider* did not scream out as the orange fire bathed him. Though his clothing caught fire, he did not. Instead, he merely threw himself forward, seemingly into the very path of the multiple beams seeking his life. Dropping low, between the slowly swinging arcs, he rolled across the floor, dousing most of the flames eating away at his cloak. Pulling himself quickly to cover behind a large leather couch as the terrible orange lines cut their destructive paths above his position, he took note of their directions, nodding to himself with grim satisfaction.

"Automatic sentries. Mechanical guard dogs. Very sloppy, Boss. Or should I say, Martin Basilton?'"

"No need to be so formal, Richard. We're all friends here."

Having expected to run into the very weapon being used against him there in the mansion's interior, the *Spider* had fashioned himself a defense out of several of the captured suits of armor. Taking a number of the lighter panels, he had fastened them inside his cloak. It was not meant to be an elaborate, or even lasting defense, but he knew it would give him the element of surprise he would need sooner or later.

Also, knowing all too well that his makeshift defense would only protect him once or twice at best from the Accursed Light, he had also come prepared to minimize its effects. Reaching into the webbed vest hidden beneath his cloak, he pulled forth a large, flexible rubber container. As the mechanized firing system sent the orange fire flashing through the living room once more, he tossed the packet upward into the spot where several of the searing rays would intersect.

At the moment the searing beams sparked against the container, it exploded with a violent fury, filling the room with a wildly expanding ball of fire followed by a thickly voluminous cloud of smoke. The oily black haze rushed in all directions, immediately obscuring the mansion's series of cameras and two-way mirrors.

"Excellent," came the Boss's voice once more. "But, what else could we expect from the Master of Men?" The filtered voice paused, then added;

"You know, it was our paper that first called you that. Ahhhhh, my yes, the *Spider* and his delightful bag of tricks. Filling a room with smoke so as to affect an escape. I would applaud, but I suspect you might detect a rather obviously disingenuous note in the display."

The *Spider* did not choose to answer. Nor did the Boss speak again. Not immediately. As the bilious darkness created by the collision of the orange beams with a bag of gasoline and oil spread further, the Accursed Light projectors were shut down. A fearsome silence permeated the mansion at that point, punctuated only by the crackling of the various fires ironically set by the place's own defenses and the quiet rhythmic bubbling of the pump used to filter the water in the room's large central fish tank. As the seconds dragged along, the Boss's voice rang out once more.

"Really now, this silence of yours is tiresome. Let us discuss this as gentlemen should. Seriously, you must know that I fully expected this meeting to take place eventually."

Ignoring the voice attempting to engage him in conversation, the *Spider* had managed to crawl beneath his still spreading blanket of smoke to a wall where he had spotted one of the Boss's cameras. Having not a second to spare, he first slid a pair of filters into his nostrils, then turned the blade still in his hand to the task of prying open the shielding plate protecting the device. As he did so, the Boss spoke once more, announcing;

"I knew you were not dead, back in December. After all, how could Richard Wentworth, the *Spider*, slay the *Spider*? And please, don't bother to protest. Really, your so-called secret identity is the most poorly kept confidence in all the city—you must realize that." When his question was met with further silence, the Boss sighed, then continued, saying;

"I will admit to having become a trifle concerned when one month, then two, then three all passed by with no resurfacing of New York's noble, long-suffering hero. After certain details of my timetable forced me to begin my campaign, and you worked the streets against me like any commoner, when the *Spider* remained steadfastly dead, I will admit that I did become concerned. I mean, let's face facts, no one likes to admit when they're wrong."

Finally forcing the panel free, Wentworth bent himself to the task of pulling the camera forward so as to expose its power cable. Without hesitation, he sliced the device free from the wires connected to it, then threw the camera aside so that he might begin peeling back the protective insulation from around the individual filaments.

"But then, here you are, back again. Restored. Whole and hail. Ready to hear my offer."

Taking interest in the slightest lilt in the Boss's voice, the *Spider* paused, not answering the mechanical voice emitting from the various speakers placed about the mansion, but waiting to hear what it might say next.

"Join me ... unite your efforts to my own. Help me transform this world."

Not believing he would hear anything that could possibly sway his mind, but always willing to give an adversary the benefit of the doubt, if for no other reason than personal amusement, the *Spider* took several short, rapid breaths, clearing his lungs and sinus passages. Not wishing to reveal his position, but curious to see if the sound of his voice might attract a new barrage of orange fire, Wentworth shouted his answer using the methods of a stage ventriloquist, causing his words to appear to be coming from the other side of the room.

"Why would I do such a thing?"

"Because ultimately, you and I, we want the same things. We both wish to see a better world, a more orderly world, one where man's baser instincts are curbed. I've spent years, using the shield of the journalist's curiosity to gather the necessary information to build a force powerful enough to terrorize this sick and brutal planet of ours into behaving itself. But, building an army, and leading them, those are two completely different things."

"Indeed they are, Basilton," replied the *Spider*. Having finished stripping away enough insulation from the camera's wires, the avenger scanned the area once more. As best he could see through the cloud cover he had created, none of the Boss's soldiers had been sent forward to find him.

"Perhaps he actually means this offer of his." Wondering how such could be justified against other things he had been told, the *Spider* questioned;

"Your offer is a bit hard to believe. After all, it seems odd you would attempt to murder the fiancée of the man you believe me to be if you actually wanted me to join your cause."

The *Spider's* accusation was followed by a brief pause. Finally, however, the Boss answered him, saying;

"Sorry. Wasn't aware you knew about that." The electronic voice was muffled for a moment, a sign the *Spider* took to mean Basilton had paused to give orders to some of his men. Preparing himself for an onslaught, Wentworth pulled at the wires, straining to jerk them further from the wall when the Boss's distorted voice returned again, saying;

"Yes, you're right, of course. Just a clumsy attempt to stall you while I moved my men into place." The voice went silent for a moment once more, and then, just as the *Spider* yanked free a great length of the cable from the wall, it spoke once more, announcing;

"But, since they are in place, I bid you *adieu*, Richard. I do believe it is time someone killed the *Spider* for real."

And with those words, even as Wentworth wrapped the end of the wires around a small grenade to give them weight, a score of men moved into the lower level of the mansion, all of them armed with yet another weapon from the *Spider's* past.

But unlike the Accursed Light, this was one against which he had brought no defense!

31

RAM SINGH stepped out onto the open air platform surrounding the torch held on high in the right hand of Lady Liberty. From every direction below him, police officers fired into the air, sending bullets from pistols and rifles as well as shotgun rounds at the twin airships. Impressive as the amount of firepower was which they sent against the blimps, however, none of it seemed to have any effect.

By the time Jackson arrived on the observation deck as well, Singh had already unloaded everything he felt he needed from his duffle. Seeing a shred-edged grapple within his comrade's hand, as well as several score of yards worth of the *Spider's* Web—the light-weight, ultra-thin but extremely strong rope created by the late Professor Brownlee—attached to it, Jackson blinked hard, then shouted over the mixed sounds of wind and gunfire;

"You, sir, if you don't mind me saying so, are one decidedly crazy bastard!"

"To the contrary, I know my father quite well," answered the Sikh. Dropping the grapple end of his line over the edge of the platform, he turned his head so his eyes might meet his friend's as he added;

"But I must admit, in all honesty, I am most certain he would find himself in agreement with the remainder of your statement."

Jackson nodded toward Singh even as he pulled his Army radio up to his head. Getting Carpenter once more, he insisted the police halt their barrage, citing that if for no other reason, they were having no effect whatsoever. He did not want to mention the fact that his comrade was about to make an assault on one of the blimps for fear those piloting the craft could possibly have their own radios with which they might be monitoring their enemy's conversations. Still, not to leave Carpenter completely in the dark, he told the sergeant;

"We'll try throwing a bowl of curry at them, see if that does anything."

Jackson could hear the slight hesitation in Carpenter's voice, knew he had confused the officer somewhat with his reference. Then, just as quickly, the sergeant called for a cease fire, chuckling as he told Jackson;

"I do believe I read you letter perfect, mister. You go ahead and give 'em heartburn for me."

As the gunfire from below thinned, then disappeared, Singh continued his preparations. More than three hundred feet in the air, he let out nearly two score feet of line, then began twirling his grapple in great, swooping arcs. Around and around the iron mass flew, Singh's great muscles straining as he continuing to let out more line even as the airships drew closer. Then, when the first of the blimps was almost overhead, he snapped his wrist and sent the grapple hurtling directly at it. The barbed edges sank into the rubberized cloth of the ship's outer skin, holding fast when the Sikh tested the line.

Without a word, Singh wrapped the *Spider*'s Web around his gloved left hand, reaching upward with his right to grab hold and then pull himself up and over the edge of the observation platform. At the same time, however, a further gust of wind moved the blimp unexpectedly sideways, jerking Singh up and over the edge.

Jackson had meant to hold onto the end of the line, to secure it around the platform's railing to aid his friend's ascent, but it was too late. In a single second Ram Singh had been pulled some twenty feet away from the platform. He now hung, sixty feet below the airship, swaying wildly in the breeze. Helpless to aid his companion, Jackson watched the Sikh swinging erratically at the end of the line, unable for the moment, because of the blimp's sudden violent motion, to do much more other than hang on desperately.

And then, as Jackson stared in horror, a large panel began to slide open along the bottom of the airship's gondola. From his vantage point in the torch he could see clearly that it would only be seconds before their foes would be in position and, that when they were, they would be able to see Ram Singh hanging from the bottom of their vessel!

STARING through the thinning haze of gasoline and oil smoke still present, the *Spider* recognized the weapons of the approaching thugs instantly. They were a type of rifle which fired over-sized shells containing a payload of extremely corrosive acid.

"That's right, Richard. I could have sent in men with guns. But that would be so ... ordinary. Unworthy of your great efforts. You, of all people, do not deserve such a simple, routine death. No, the master of men, he deserves a heroic passing. One filled with agony and torment. Something out of an opera. Something worthy of Dante."

The *Spider* ignored Basilton's voice, using his keen hearing instead to locate the Boss's men. Both sides of the conflict were equally blinded due to the still smoldering fires. But, the *Spider* had one advantage—since the arrival of the thugs, he had not moved, had made no noise since their entrance into the area. Knowing his time to act effectively was running out, however, he took a deep breath, then went into action.

Reaching once more into the webbed vest hidden

beneath his cloak, he pulled forth the second and last of his rubber containers. Holding it in one hand, he gathered the length of wire he had ripped from the wall in the other, careful not to touch the exposed ends. Then, when he sensed none of the approaching thugs were looking in his direction, he let fly with the container, sending it toward the ceiling above the greatest concentration of the Boss's men. At the same time, he hurled the end of the weighted wires at Basilton's grand fish tank.

"It's him! Fire—kill him!"

Numerous things happened within the massive living room at the same time. Four of the thugs who could actually make out the *Spider*'s form through the smoke fired their weapons in his direction. The grenade dragging the camera wires through the air hit the fish tank and shattered its side. The rubber bag reached a spot directly above the Boss's men and began to fall. And lastly, the *Spider* pulled his .45s as pandemonium fell on the Basilton mansion.

Two of the acid shells burst against the *Spider*. He had taken the risk of exposing himself, counting on the armor in his cloak to allow him to survive at least a first barrage. As the acid hissed, disintegrating the fabric of his cape with an unbelievable speed, the armor kept the overwhelming majority of it from reaching his skin, but only because he immediately shrugged his way out of it. Before it could touch the floor, however, the world crashed in on his foes.

First, the wires wrapped around the grenade were soaked by the escaping waters of the fish tank. Instantly the power went out throughout the mansion. With the sun still not quite risen, suddenly the Boss's men were plunged into an utterly smoke-filled darkness, one shattered when the *Spider* took his first shots, riddling his rubber bag with bullets.

Gasoline and oil rained down upon the men, splashing in every direction, igniting as it came in contact with the dozens of small patches still burning within the room. Men screamed as their skin crisped and their hair burned. Chaos filled the area as the new fires blazed up and out of control, sending spectral shadows dancing across the darkness. Several of the thugs gave orders, shouting for their fellows to calm themselves, to help extinguish the new fires, but they were too late.

"You men have, all of you, wasted your lives." Aiming at the closest of the Boss's men, the *Spider* said;

"Now, I shall end them."

Two of the thugs began to turn in the direction of the *Spider*'s voice, only to find themselves knocked from their feet by a pair of .45 slugs each. Head and body, head and body, the *Spider* continued the slaughter, managing to eliminate twelve of the thugs before coming up empty. Ejecting his clips, he reloaded, taking in his surroundings as he did so.

The entire living room was on fire now, thick smoke rolling throughout the house. All of the men sent in with the acid guns were either down or in retreat. The threads in Basilton's wall-to-wall carpeting had proved highly flammable, encouraging what might have only been an easily containable blaze into an all-consuming inferno. Finding himself beginning to choke despite his nose filters, the *Spider* thought;

"Discretion, valor, better part ... yes, I do believe it is that time."

Seeing the closest exit as being the one through which he had first entered, the *Spider* raced for the now ruined front door and leaped through it, tucking and rolling out onto the front lawn. He had meant to make as difficult a target as possible of himself, but he need not have bothered. The Boss's men were in complete disarray. Those who had escaped the downstairs confrontation were for the most part sprawled on the damp lawn, coughing and choking, the fight completely rung out of them. Those others in evidence were simply running away.

"Rats and sinking ships," mused the *Spider*, watching the cowards racing off against the first rays of the coming morning sun. "There's an old story. But ... what about your fearless leader?"

Catching his own breath, the *Spider* suddenly realized he was making an obvious target of himself. Stepping back against the front wall of the Boss's mansion, he thought for a moment, deciding on a plan of action. Having studied the grounds as best he could before entering, he was aware that the Basilton property extended back for a number of acres. Remembering that all access drives came in from behind the mansion, the *Spider* realized that unlike his troops, the Boss would most likely attempt to escape his blazing home from the rear where his garages were positioned.

Realizing that the mansion was of such a great size that by the time he ran to either end he might possibly miss Basilton's exit, the *Spider* pulled the length of his web which he always carried with him and quickly lassoed one of the burning home's many chimneys. Scaling the front of the mansion in seconds, the *Spider* made his way to the uppermost point of the roof just in time to spot the Boss—

Climbing into the passenger seat of a twin engine plane, one just small enough to take off from the private airstrip located behind his burning home!

32

"**C**LIMB, DAMN YOU!" Ram Singh sneered his words, cursing his own efforts. "Old, pathetic, worthless dung beetle—*climb!*"

The Sikh's progress thus far had been steady, but slow, the combination of his body weight and his efforts to ascend the *Spider*'s Web unanchored keeping him in a wildly swinging pattern which cut his speed to a minimum. On the other hand, those riding within the airship he was trying to reach had not been able to get a clear shot at him because of his gyrations. They had also been prevented from taking careful aim because of Jackson.

The former military man, knowing he was being assigned the high ground that morning, had automatically made a high-powered rifle with a strong sight part of his kit. Protected by the steel and copper of Lady Liberty's torch, he was perfectly positioned to keep those on the blimp from getting a clear shot at Singh by laying down protective fire.

"Faster," the Sikh ordered himself, his voice hissing through his teeth. "Hand over hand, climb! Men deserving of death are waiting for you to release them from this world—now *climb!*"

With every upward reach Singh gained another yard. The muscles of his arms and shoulders were aching, but he ignored the pain. All his fingers were cramping, but he paid their agony no attention.

How could he do such, he asked himself. Was he a woman? Should he take care not to break a nail?

Chuckling at his own humor, the Sikh noted that he had already passed the half-way point. The sound of bullets raced past him in both directions, but he afforded them no attention. The Boss's men were shooting at him. Jackson, most likely, was shooting back at them. To think on such things was a waste of time. He was in a battle. Such were the things that happened during battles. To Singh, such trifles did not matter.

All that mattered was the mission before him. He could see it clearly. And the completion of it was within sight, mere feet from his grasp.

Smiling, the Sikh ignored the whispers within his brain warning him that his strength was failing, that his fingers were going stiff. In his heart, he knew they would suffice. They would take him to his goal. In seconds, he would reach the outer skin of the blimp, of that there was no question.

And *then* ... then he would know either victory or defeat, which was all that mattered!

THE *SPIDER* stood at the apex of Basilton's home, struggling to catch his breath. Flames were licking their way up all sides of the mansion. Although it had thus far resisted the inferno, there was little doubt the roof would be engulfed soon as well. As he surveyed the scene before him, Wentworth, a pilot himself, worked out how much area the small twin motor below him would need to take off. As best he could tell, luck might be offering him one last good hand.

As impressive as was the size of Basilton's estate, to have put in a runway capable of allowing a plane a straight take off would have been absurdly wasteful. Thus the publisher had installed a half-run, a thin strip with a large circle at its far end, somewhat resembling a flattened thermometer. A plane used such a runway to get its engine's warmed and to build an opening pace. The over-sized circle at the end allowed a pilot to maintain much of their building speed, after which take-off would be possible after a return run down the strip.

As the *Spider* watched the plane start to move away from him toward the circle, he began to feel the results of his efforts so far. For the first time since the battle had begun he had a moment to take stock. The first thing he noticed was that two acid stripes had burned him severely—one across his left wrist, the other a searing hole drilled into his right shoulder. As burns on his back, legs and the side of his head began to throb, he realized he had not escaped the touch of the Accursed Light completely, either.

"Pull yourself together, Wentworth," the *Spider*'s voice hissed within his mind. "Cast off your weakness. Stand straight. Have you come this far to surrender now?"

For a moment, his mind offered him different paths he might follow. Basilton, after all, was well known. They had the all the proof they needed to hold him wherever he surfaced. His assets would be seized. Even if he escaped momentarily, he asked himself, what of it? The threat of the man was over. He had been stopped. Neutralized. The affair was over.

"Haven't you done enough?"

The question whispered itself quietly through Wentworth's mind. After all, he asked himself, weren't you going to give this existence all up anyway? Didn't you decide you had done your part? Why risk your life now when it's all over? What reason could there be?

Nita—

Without hesitation, the *Spider* ran for the far end of the mansion, racing along the now burning rooftop as the Boss's plane roared back down the runway. Measuring each step, his keen eye concentrating on watching the plane, gauging its speed, knowing he needed to make his move at exactly the right split second, the *Spider* threw himself through the last wall of fire, then hurled himself off the mansion's roof as the escaping twin motor took to the air!

A*LLAH BE PRAISED*. Ram Singh hung desperately against the side of the airship. He had reached the point where his grapple had snagged the outer skin, a spot taking him out of range of those who had been attempting to shoot him from the gondola. Since he could still hear shots being fired, however, he knew that Jackson must have continued to engage the thugs. The Sikh realized that his friend might also be pinned down by their gunfire as well, trapped for having tried to help Singh.

"Enough time wasted, wastrel," he told himself. One gloved hand wrapped around the *Spider*'s Web, with his other the Sikh pulled forth his great sword, shouting;

"How can you think of rest when there are souls in need of being sent to *Hell?!*"

With a powerful thrust Singh sliced through the outer cloth skin of the blimp. Despite his bravado, the great Sikh knew his strength was failing him. Desperation forcing his hand, he tore open a massive hole in the side of the airship and then tumbled inward, sliding down to the bottom of the blimp's aluminum framework.

"Praise all my ancestors," he muttered weakly, sprawled out on the airship's cloth bottom, his back resting against the main spine strut of the blimp.

His body aching in every joint, the climb he had endured an effort greater than almost any other man might match, still Ram Singh pushed his way up off the rubberized cloth. Though his entire body screamed for relief, he knew he could afford it none. He could still hear gunfire, but had no idea at that point who was doing the shooting or what might be their target. He could taste blood in his mouth, although he could not fathom how he had taken such an injury.

Out of all the things he did not know, what Singh *did* know that morning, however, was that the Boss's men were there to complete a mission, and that if they were to be thwarted, he had to act, and act immediately.

Reaching deep within himself, Singh pushed, straining himself to the utmost, forcing himself up. Hands and knees. Then on his knees alone. One knee only. And finally, grasping the ribbing next to him, with an effort beyond even the dreams of most men ... he stood. Though desperate for relief, he did not hesitate, did not think. For the Sikh, the time for planning had long passed. Now, there were only two possibilities—death or victory.

Running toward the center of the ship, sword in hand, he saw the hatch from the gondola begin to open. As he ran faster, trying to close the gap, he saw the muzzles of automatic weapons being shoved through the opening. Then, as he drew directly on top of the portal, the Boss's men opened fire!

THE *SPIDER* slammed against the tail of the escaping plane, his fingers desperately grasping for any handhold. His left hand found nothing, but his right fist smashed against one of the twin motor's small observation windows, shattering the glass and giving him a tenuous handhold. From the inside, he could hear excited voices shouting. As footsteps banged toward the rear of the plane, the *Spider* pulled one of his .45s and jammed it against the skin of the aircraft, shouting;

"Die—*all* of you!"

Without hesitation the black-garbed avenger pulled the trigger over and over, moving the barrel with each shot, sending bullets ricocheting throughout the interior of the aircraft. Not willing to risk missing any of those inside, no thought given to his own safety, glass from the broken window slicing through his arm, the *Spider* dropped his empty .45, pulled another, and then fired again.

Screams filled the air for a moment, after which the only sounds that could be heard were those of the plane's engines. The *Spider* took several rapid breaths, trying to orient himself, and then his throat closed and his eyes went wide as he felt the twin motor lurch violently. For whatever reason, he did not know, but suddenly the plane had lost its upward trajectory and had doubled back toward the Earth.

The plane, its pilot dead, was headed back to the ground on a deadly collision course at top speed. And hanging outside for dear life, there was nothing the *Spider* could do to prevent it!

A T first sight of the gun muzzles coming from below, Ram Singh had launched himself into the air directly at the opening hatch. Although the Boss's henchmen managed to get off more than a dozen shots, only one struck the Sikh, and that merely a glancing tear along his thigh. Landing on top of the hatch with his full weight, however, he crushed the wrist of one thug, and the forearms of two others.

As the trio dropped their weapons, screaming in pain, Singh rolled off the bent hatch and then threw it open. Pulling a large wad of spittle together in his mouth, he spat it into the face of the thug in the middle, bringing back his great blade as he shouted;

"You are dogs yapping the cries of the cowardly, and my ears would know silence."

With one motion his sword flew, slicing off the top of one man's head, cutting two thirds of the way through the other. Not hesitating, he kicked the third man back inside while he wrenched his sword free, then dropped down inside the gondola itself, landing upright despite the searing pain of his wound.

Within the cabin he found only two others, both of whom seemed to be needed to pilot the blimp. Crossing to the hatch from which only minutes earlier the trio now on the floor had been trying to murder him, Singh flipped the portal open, then kicked the closest of the wounded thugs through it. Without hesitation, he followed suit with the second and then the third, sending all three to their deaths, their bodies smashing against the island far below.

Immediately turning toward the pilot and navigator, giving them no time to think he asked;

"And, would you care to join your fellows?"

When both screamed out for mercy, Singh grinned, then told them what they needed to do if they truly wished to earn more than a handful of seconds of further existence!

KNOWING he had only moments to act, the *Spider* slammed his body as best he could against the section of the plane wall through which he had fired. The light-weight material, already severely damaged, caved in under the pressure of his attack. Pulling himself inside, the *Spider* surveyed the interior of the aircraft quickly to see what he was up against. What he saw gave him hope. The two toughs the Boss had brought with him had been slaughtered by his hail of gunfire. The pilot as well had died, his collapsed form being what had thrown the plane into its downward trajectory. Indeed, only Basilton himself had survived. Seeing the *Spider* enter the plane, the publisher wailed;

"Richard, save us!"

Staggering forward, the *Spider* made it to the small twin motor's control section. Jerking the pilot's body free, he tossed the useless flesh aside, and then bent to the problem of straightening out the aircraft's rapid descent, mindfully keeping at least the corner of his eye on Basilton.

He need not have worried. The once powerful Boss had been reduced to a frightened, crying annoyance. Curled in a ball, he lie huddled against the side of the airship, still screaming for Wentworth to stop them from crashing even after the plane had been leveled off for several minutes. The *Spider* had allowed him to continue on for several reasons.

One, he needed to rest, to catch his breath, to brace himself against the pain he knew was going to make itself felt throughout his body. Now that the battle had been won, the threat of the Boss and his seemingly invincible forces destroyed, his body would stop ignoring the tremendous amounts of damage it had taken.

Second, he saw no reason to comfort his foe. The man had planned the subjugation of the entire world. He had thought to make all men his slaves, not because he was in any way better or deserving, but simply because he thought he might be able to get away with it.

And the third reason he allowed Basilton to whimper and scream in fear of his death was because of Nita. His beloved, still unconscious, still hovering at death's door. Perhaps never to know he had planned to give everything up for her. Never to truly know how much she meant to him. How much he needed her. How much he loved her.

After several minutes, however, Basilton realized that the *Spider* must have righted the plane. Going quiet, opening his fingers enough so that he might see through them, he squeaked in desperate excitement;

"You did it, you did it. We're not going to die."

His voice tired and dark, each syllable growled with a weary hatred, the *Spider* answered;

"All men die, Basilton."

"Yes, yes," agreed the would-be conqueror. "Obviously, of course. But not today—yes? Not today."

Looking over at the publisher, his tear-stained face alive with glee, the *Spider* pulled one of his .45s, and said;

"Wrong again, madman."

EPILOGUE

"**H**OW does it feel to be heroes, fellahs?"

Ram Singh and Jackson stood on the southernmost shore of Manhattan, surrounded by police officers and reporters. Thousands had witnessed the battle above the Statue of Liberty. By the time Singh had forced the crew of the blimp he had captured to ram its opposite number, the entire area had become packed to bursting with spectators.

"Ohhh, I don't know," said Jackson modestly, "we didn't do all that much."

The two airships had become entangled, and then forced to the ground when Singh had taken it upon himself to slice open the two massive airbags within his blimp. None were injured, the descent of the ruined airships was so slow, but none escaped, either. With hundreds of police officers there on the island, and aboard the boats closing in on it, those remaining of the Boss's forces surrendered without hesitation.

"What'dya you say, big guy," one reporter asked of Singh. "You as humble as your buddy here?"

Wentworth, upon landing the Boss's plane, had gone to a phone immediately and called Kirkpatrick. Confirming their suspicions of Basilton, and the fact he was no more, the commissioner had swung into instantaneous action. Squadrons of police were sent to all properties belonging to Basilton, *The City Bugle*, as well as others it was suspected Basilton may have rented through operatives. Ever since he and Wentworth had proved to themselves that someone connected to the paper had sponsored the field trip to the upstate college—the one which had ended so disastrously for that small group of young women only days earlier— police detectives had been assigned to trace ownership or occupancy of any structures possibly connected to Basilton. A judge friendly with Kirkpatrick had made certain search warrants were plentiful.

"Whether I am humble is not for me to decide. What we did this day, would not any man do? I am but pleased to have been able to serve this truly great democracy which I have made my home."

Kirkpatrick, who had been raced to the end of the island once it was clear he could safely come out of hiding, called for a round of applause for both Singh and Jackson. He praised their efforts, as well of those as their employer, Richard Wentworth. With every news outlet in the city present, the commissioner thanked his long time friend for giving over his home as a secondary headquarters from which he could fight the Boss in secret.

"Richard Wentworth is the kind of man this city needs. He gave freely all his resources so this monster known now to be one of our most 'upstanding citizens' could be brought low."

When some in the throng asked about the possibility of Wentworth being the *Spider*, Kirkpatrick scoffed at them, reminding them that he himself had witnessed his friend sending the despised masked vigilante to his death. He also swore that he and Wentworth had been in constant contact since he had taken up residence at Sutton Place to play out the subterfuge of his supposed death.

"The *Spider* is no more," the commissioner assured the crowd. "In a city as bustling as ours, something that happened three months ago should be ancient history. Forgotten. Indeed, as long as New York has brave men such as mister Ram Singh and his comrade Ronald Jackson here, or my own Sergeant Thomas Carpenter, who was responsible for coordinating all of our efforts today, what need have we of masked men?"

The crowd cheered the obvious sentiment. Then, as more questions were about to be asked, someone in the crowd noticed that Singh's leg was bleeding. The Sikh protested, saying of the tear caused by the bullet which had grazed his leg;

"Bahhh, this? Tis nothing but a scratch."

But Kirkpatrick wisely used the wound as a means for easing Wentworth's men out of the limelight. He knew them both well enough to understand that neither was the type to wish for praise or accolades. He knew they wished to return to Sutton Place, to check on their employer, and their friend.

Over the following few days, the two would be called upon to accept awards, attend dinners, and even make speeches. Much would be made around the world of the fact that the man who saved the Statue of Liberty was not an American citizen. Guilelessly, Singh would announce that he did not know one had to do anything but believe in democracy to be an American.

He and Jackson would become the focus of the city's, and the nation's, attention for roughly eleven days, and then other news would relegate them to the backwaters populated by those whose notoriety had passed.

As for the Boss, himself, it would be proved after his various arsenals had been uncovered, that his entire plot had been a sham. He had not nearly enough resources to attack cities around the world. In fact, his available capital had been stretched thin merely attacking New York. His entire plan, as testimony from eventually captured lieutenants from his organization proved, had revolved around the fact he considered people cowards, desperate to keep their comforts. He had expected country after country to surrender out of terror of losing what they had, out of fear over the thought of standing up on their own two feet.

"With the wars in both Europe and the Pacific raging," Kirkpatrick told the crowds more than once over the following days, "with morale evaporating everywhere, who's to say he might not have succeeded if not for the brave resistance this city showed him?"

As for Richard Wentworth himself, the actual ramrod that had stoked that resistance, he shunned the limelight. He made the obligatory appearance for the press, but only one, and only long enough to announce that he was no hero. He was glad to have helped, but that outside of a little detective work, he had only managed to get himself blown up.

Then, with the fourth estate placated, and the world looking in directions other than his own, Richard Wentworth had retreated into his home and closed the door. He did have wounds which needed care, and scars which had to heal, but the worst of them were not physical.

Richard Wentworth was a man well accustomed to pain. He had been shot and stabbed repeatedly. His body had been beaten, his teeth loosened, his bones broken. He had undergone grueling tortures of a hundred varieties. None such agony had mattered. He had been slowed in his time, forestalled, even crippled—but never stopped.

Not until that moment when the Boss's thugs had exploded their device beneath the assembly hall. Not until Nita Van Sloan had been pulverized and crushed.

Not until the woman he loved had been dragged closer to death than any human being could be without either recovering, or passing beyond.

And thus, as parties and dinners were held in Jackson and Singh's honor, as Kirkpatrick continued to explain away all that had happened, as the death machines were collected and destroyed, as the city began the laborious task of rebuilding, Richard Wentworth ignored it all.

Day after day, as life continued for others, he sat in the same chair, quietly watching the shallow breathing of the woman he loved. He watched her lips, hoping for the slightest tremor that might indicate she was about to speak. He watched her eyes, desperate for even the simple fluttering that might indicate she was dreaming.

And every so often, he would ask her the question he had been prevented from asking her the night of his birthday.

"Nita Van Sloan ... will you marry me?"

And every time he did so, when she did not answer, when she simply continued to breathe—shallowly, weakly—then he would return to simply watching—

And wiping his eyes, which for some reason, he could not keep dry.